FOOTBALL
SHORTS

This collection first published 2012 by Walker Books Ltd
87 Vauxhall Walk, London SE11 5HJ

This edition published 2013

10 9 8 7 6 5 4 3 2 1

Anthology © 2012 Tom Watt
"A Quick One-Two" © 2012 Tomáš Rosický
"Letting Go" © 2012 Nick Hornby
"Decisions, Decisions" © 2012 Alan Sefton
"Trials & Tribulations" © 2012 Curtis Davies
"Deal or No Deal?" © 2012 Matt Holland
"Murder at Manor Park!" © 2012 Tom Palmer
"One Katy Jackson" © 2012 Faye White
"Disappeared" © 2012 Hilary Freeman
"A Clean Sheet" © 2012 Vincent Kompany
"The Final Whistle" © 2012 Terry Deary
"The Angels of Peru" © 2012 Mal Peet
"Bury Away" © 2012 Alan Davies
Various poems © 2012 Paul Cookson
Illustrations © 2012 Mark Long

The moral rights of the contributors have been asserted

This book has been typeset in Scala Informal,
Gill Sans and Journal Text

Printed and bound in Great Britain by Clays Ltd, St Ives plc

All rights reserved. No part of this book may be
reproduced, transmitted or stored in an information
retrieval system in any form or by any means, graphic,
electronic or mechanical, including photocopying,
taping and recording, without prior written permission
from the publisher.

British Library Cataloguing in Publication Data:
a catalogue record for this book is available from
the British Library

ISBN 978-1-4063-4511-7

www.walker.co.uk

FOOTBALL SHORTS

Edited by TOM WATT
Illustrated by MARK LONG

WALKER
BOOKS

CONTENTS

INTRODUCTION

Shelby Town are a fictional football team who play in the real-life Barclays Premier League. They're also the team that feature – one way or another – in all the stories you're about to read. Town have a bit in common with a lot of real clubs, like Wigan, Blackburn, Norwich and Reading, to name just a few.

Shelby is a town somewhere in the middle of England, halfway between London and Birmingham. Supporting Town has been pretty exciting lately. Fifteen years ago, they were playing non-league football in the old Vauxhall Conference. Like at so many smaller clubs, money was tight and the players were semi-professional. But then a local businessman, Ernest Carstairs, bought the club, paid off its debts and gave the manager some money to spend on the team. Since then, Shelby Town haven't looked back. Under boss Mick Diamond, they climbed through the divisions and then, a couple of years ago, won the Championship Play-Off Final at Wembley.

The hero at Wembley was the club's longest-serving player, skipper Dave Morgan. Town taking a place in the

Premier League was a dream come true for Dave and for everyone connected with the club.

Mick Diamond trusted the boys who'd got Town promoted, but he brought in a couple of overseas stars to strengthen the squad: French midfielder Jean-Pierre Vert and Nigerian striker Dotun Odegbame. And lads like Stuart Dolan come through from the youth team to make their mark in the Premier League too.

Against all the odds – and despite the pundits saying they were relegation certainties – Shelby Town survived. In fact, that first season in the Premier League the club reached the Carling Cup final.

You may have read about Town – and the personalities behind the scenes – in the Double Club English and Maths textbooks used in many schools in recent years.

It's been an incredible journey for the players, the staff and the fans: for everyone at Shelby Town, in fact, including Ernest, Mick, Dave, Dotun, Stuart and Jean-Pierre. Now read on. The story's only just begun…

TEAM SHEET

TOM WATT

Tom Watt is an actor who also writes books.
Mostly about football. His last big one was called
2010: When the World Cup Came to South Africa.
He invented the club in *Football Shorts*, Shelby
Town, for some textbooks he wrote for the Double
Club programme for schools. He writes regularly
for the Arsenal match programme and is currently
working on a football-based feature film.

VINCENT KOMPANY

Vincent Kompany was born in Uccle in Belgium
and started his career at Anderlecht, where he
played for three years before moving to Hamburg
in Germany. In 2008 he joined his current team,
Manchester City, and won the Premier League
with them in 2012. Vincent is currently captain of
both City and Belgium and is a FIFA Ambassador
for the charity SOS Children's Villages.

NICK HORNBY

Nick Hornby's *Fever Pitch*, which describes his own life growing up as an Arsenal fan, is one of the best adult novels ever written about football and was made into a very successful film. Nick has published several other equally best-selling books and screenplays, including *About a Boy*, *High Fidelity* and *Slam*, his novel about a teenage skateboarder named Sam.

TOMAS ROSICKY

Tomáš Rosický is one of the Czech Republic's most talented players ever. He was born in Prague and played for Sparta before moving to Germany, when he joined Borussia Dortmund, and then to the UK in 2005 when he signed for Arsenal. Tomáš has won nearly ninety international caps and has captained his country at both the European Championships and the World Cup.

MAL PEET

Mal Peet grew up in Norfolk, which explains why he supports Norwich City. His books have won more cups than the Canaries, like the Carnegie Medal and the Guardian Children's Fiction Prize. He's written three football novels: *Keeper*, *The Penalty* and *Exposure*. The character Paul Faustino, who features in Mal's story here, actually has his own website. Google it!

MATT HOLLAND

Matt Holland had a fantastic career as a midfielder for Bournemouth, Ipswich, Charlton and the Republic of Ireland, scoring for Ireland against Cameroon at the 2002 World Cup. It turns out that Matt is as good at talking about football as he was at playing it, so he now works as an expert pundit for just about every radio and TV station you can think of.

ALAN SEFTON

Alan Sefton has worked at Arsenal for over twenty-five years and is head of the club's award-winning community department. Based at the Emirates Stadium, Alan and his staff use football as a way to connect people of all ages and backgrounds, especially teenagers, using schemes like the Arsenal Double Club literacy programme.

CURTIS DAVIES

Curtis Davies was born in Leytonstone in London and made his debut for Luton Town when they were still in the Football League. Since then he has played for West Bromwich Albion, Aston Villa, Leicester City and Birmingham City, where he's been since 2011. Curtis made his international debut at centre half for the England Under-21s in 2006 and has been in full squads since without winning his first cap yet.

FAYE WHITE

Faye White grew up in Horley in Surrey. She plays centre back and is one of English football's most decorated players, having won nearly thirty trophies as captain of Arsenal Ladies and captaining for England at four major tournaments. Faye was awarded an MBE in 2006 for her services to football and had to retire from playing because of injury earlier this year.

ALAN DAVIES

Alan Davies is a comedian, writer and actor who is probably best known as the star of the TV detective series *Jonathan Creek* and the film *Angus, Thongs and Perfect Snogging*, as well as being a permanent panellist on the quiz show *QI*. Alan's latest book is called *Teenage Revolution* and is about growing up in the 1980s.

HILARY FREEMAN

Hilary Freeman is a writer who lives in Camden Town in North London, and she's written five novels. The latest is called *The Boy From France* and is the third in a series called Camden Town Tales. As well as writing, Hilary is an agony aunt for newspapers and magazines. As she supports Arsenal, she knows all about agony...

TOM PALMER

Tom Palmer was born in Leeds and supports Leeds United. His first novel, *Foul Play*, was shortlisted for the Blue Peter Book Award, and he is the official author of the Premier League Reading Stars scheme. Look out for *White Fear* the latest title in Tom's new series of football stories, The Squad, which is out now.

PAUL COOKSON

Paul Cookson is the poet in residence at the National Football Museum. He writes poetry for children and adults and had two new collections out last year, *Give Us a Goal!* and *Saturday Men*. Paul performs his poems live at festivals, on the radio and in thousands of schools and libraries all over the country. He also entertains audiences (and drives his family mad) by playing the ukulele.

TERRY DEARY

Terry Deary was born in Sunderland and still supports his hometown club. He has written around 200 books over the past thirty-five years, most of them for children, and is also an actor, playwright and scriptwriter. Terry is most famous for creating the Horrible Histories books, which have been made into a hugely popular TV series as well as a stage show, a computer game and even a virtual world.

A QUICK ONE-TWO

TOMAS ROSICKY

Sometimes brothers are the very best of friends. Other times they are the bitterest of rivals. But most of the time they're both. That's exactly how it always was with me and Jerry.

I should get it out of the way now, I suppose. Yes, I'm Tom. And my younger brother's Jerry. What were Mum and Dad thinking when it came to naming us? You needn't bother coming up with jokes about us being cartoon characters. We've heard them all. Actually, we heard them all a long time ago. And there were times, when we were younger, when we probably looked like Tom and Jerry, too. Chasing each other around the block of flats, getting into fights, arguing about anything and everything. That's how brothers are.

We could've been twins, everybody said. We looked so alike. Although every time Jerry grew a bit, I'd put a spurt on too, to make sure I stayed a centimetre or two taller. Anyway, together we were the Barlow Boys. Any time anybody talked about us, the chances are it was to do with one thing. Jerry and I did loads of stuff together, when he wasn't getting on my nerves at least. But what we did together more than anything was play football. School playground, down the sports centre, out on the grass in front of the flats. Even indoors if Mum wasn't looking. Anywhere, everywhere. All day, every day.

No surprise, really, that the Barlow Boys loved the game. Our dad, Mick, played for Shelby Town FC back in the 1970s, when they were still knocking around in the Midland Combination League. He was always telling us how good a player he used to be. So we'd ask him, "What were you doing playing in the Midland Combination, then?" Only joking, though: Dad's a Shelby man through and through. I don't think anybody is prouder of how far Town have come since the old non-league days.

All the while me and Jerry were growing up, Dad had his own windows business, which meant he could work his own hours. Once he realized his sons liked football, that was it. Windows came second to running our little estate team, Rosemount Rovers – "The Reds". Dad did all his coaching badges. He got the council to let us use the park for training. He got to know all the parents on the estate and managed to convince them that the best players should join us instead of going off to one of the bigger teams in town. Before we knew it, Dad's under-10s were beating all comers.

Not that winning was what it was about for Dad. Not when we were eight and nine years old. Training? Well, he just used to arrange a time and a place, then me and Jerry – and all the other kids from the estate – would turn up for a game. Two-a-side, five-a-side, seven- or eight-a-side. If you were there, you played. When it came to coaching, all I can ever remember Dad doing was showing us how to kick the ball properly. In fact, Dad used to call it out so often that it became the Rosemount Rovers catchphrase: *"Laces!"*

I loved to play and my little brother Jerry loved to play. Although he hated it when I called him "Little Brother", which obviously made me do it all the time, just to wind him up. Even if there was nobody else around and Dad was at work, we'd have a game between ourselves. Some of the biggest matches happened right there in our hallway. Mum and Dad's bedroom door was one goal and the cupboard at the end was the other. One against one, and the winner would get a free flick at the loser's ear. That hallway was Manor Park or The Emirates, Wembley or the Bernabéu.

I was only a year older than Jerry. That's what he said, anyway. Actually, it was more like fourteen months. But, like I say, he didn't want to seem like the little brother. Whatever we were doing – but especially if it was football – Jerry was always desperate to get the better of me. Sometimes he'd come flying into a tackle and I'd think, If he doesn't hurt me, he's going to hurt himself! He had to beat me, had to prove he was quicker, cleverer, better at football than I was. And that kept me on my toes.

So if it was me versus Jerry, the competition was fierce. Every now and again, of course, it would end in a scrap: Jerry used to think he could fight me as well. But it wasn't always brother against brother, and I think Jerry liked it even better when we were on the same side. When we went down to the grass out in front of the flats, the game would always be the Barlow Boys versus the rest. Jerry loved that and, to be honest, so did I. I wouldn't ever tell him to his face but my brother really was a good player. If I had the choice, I always wanted Jerry on my side.

That was the two of us, from as soon as we could walk. Mum says I even got Jerry to go in goal *before* he could walk. I don't know about that. But I do know that all my best memories of growing up are football and Jerry and me. What started out as a kickaround for the boys on the estate turned into Rosemount Rovers when I was six and Jerry was five. Dad never pushed us; he never needed to. The problem was him and Mum getting us indoors for dinner and bed. But then Shelby Town came along and turned things upside down.

• • •

I was just coming up to eleven so Jerry was almost ten. With Rosemount Rovers, it didn't matter how old or young you were; we just played. Not in a league or anything, but friendly games over in the park when Dad could get them organized. We lived for those Saturday mornings and Sunday afternoons, though, when The Reds could take on the world. Somehow or other, Dad got us some kit from somewhere so we looked the part as well. And so did he: for special occasions he used to get out his old Shelby Town tracksuit and put it on. He'd laugh and say, "You boys had better call me 'The Boss'!"

It all happened at one of those friendly games. It was a Sunday afternoon and we were playing a team from Lea Vale. Most of them were a year or two older than us, but we weren't worried about that. We got a team of eight together. There were more of them, but Dad agreed with their coach that they could just use subs whenever they wanted. We lined up, ready to go, with me and Jerry playing up front.

Sometimes when we played, it was as if me and Jerry knew what the other one was going to do before he did it. I'd make a run and, without me calling for it, the ball would suddenly be rolling into my path. Or I'd cross the ball without even looking and Jerry would be there to head it into the net. Well, against that team from Lea Vale, we had one of those games. Whatever we did seemed to come off and we both scored hat-tricks. Eventually, they put on a couple of extra players just to make the game a bit more even.

I'd already lost count of the score by half-time. We all gathered around Dad as he handed out bottles of water. He didn't really say anything; he didn't need to – just asked us if we were enjoying ourselves. Before any of us could answer, the other team's coach came over and tapped Dad on the shoulder. They walked a little way away from us. Watching out of the corner of my eye, I could see Dad nodding at what the man was saying and then both of them started laughing.

After the game, Dad took us all out for a meal on the High Street. He'd never done that before. I knew we'd played well but he must have dug into his savings for pizzas and ice creams for eight, mustn't he? He had this big smile on his face that lasted all the way home. But when I asked him what was going on, he just told me to mind my own business and then ruffled my hair.

Well, a couple of days later we found out what'd happened at the game, although, by then, me and Jerry had forgotten all about it. A letter came in the post, addressed to me.

I opened it and straight away saw it had the Shelby Town club badge at the top of the page. I called out to Mum and Dad and they came through to the lounge. Shelby Town were inviting me along to Manor Park to play in a special practice game, where they were going to choose boys to join the under-12s squad at the academy. The letter said they'd had very good reports about me from a local coach they knew.

I could see by the look on Dad's face how proud he was, and I was really excited as well. But I had this funny feeling that it wasn't all good news. At bedtime, I showed Jerry the letter and he burst out crying. Not that he wasn't happy for me; he said he was. But he was heartbroken, too. The idea of me going off to play football and him not being there? He couldn't handle that at all. He said it felt like he'd never get the chance to play with me again. I tried to explain that it was only a trial and I might not get in, and even if I did, I'd still want to play out in front of the flats every day. But Jerry just pulled the covers over his head and told me he wanted to go to sleep.

I could tell that Jerry was lying there thinking. I was lying there thinking as well. Should I turn Shelby Town down? I couldn't even if I'd wanted to. Dad would've been really upset; they were his team, after all. But I hated seeing Jerry so unhappy. I didn't want to let him down either. I lay in bed, staring at the orange light from the streetlamps glowing behind the curtains. I don't know how long it took me to get to sleep but, by the time I did, I'd decided what we'd do.

Mum said she was too nervous to come and didn't want to put me off. She probably meant she fancied a couple of hours of peace and quiet around the house. Whatever: me, Dad and Jerry drove down to Manor Park early. Very, very early. Dad said I shouldn't blow my chances by being late before I'd even kicked a ball. But an hour before kick-off? Well, at least it gave me and Jerry time to go over our plan. In whispers, obviously, because we couldn't let Dad know. He'd find out soon enough.

It was fantastic. The Shelby Town youth coaches were at the ground to meet us. We went through to the first team dressing room and I started getting changed. They'd laid out kit for all of us. It was as if we were professional players for the day. I recognized a couple of the other boys from Rosemount Rovers games. I could see how nervous they were, and they could probably see how nervous I was. One of the coaches split us up into teams; they had all our names and positions. Then we went out onto the pitch to warm up.

They'd put out moveable goals on the edge of the two penalty areas, so we didn't play on a full-sized pitch. But it felt like Wembley: playing in a proper stadium, in front of a crowd, even if it was just a couple of hundred parents and friends. And Jerry and Dad. I gave Little Brother the thumbs up and he waved back.

The game kicked off and I played up front. It was hard. All the other boys were good players: the best, I suppose, from their schools and their Sunday teams. One of the defenders I was playing against towered over me. Surely he couldn't be the same age as the rest of us? I just got my head down and played. I didn't score but I set up a goal for the boy who was playing left wing. It felt like I was doing OK. The side I was playing for were 2–1 down at half-time.

During the break, while we got a drink on the side of the pitch, I looked over and saw Dad, sitting with some other parents and grinning from ear to ear. I didn't know if that was because I was playing well or because he was just proud I was playing at the ground where he had twenty years before. I gave him a wave and then saw Jerry, sitting behind him with a "Well, what d'you reckon?" look on his face. I winked at him and then ran on to start the second half.

We equalized almost straight away. The boy on the left wing crossed the ball in low and I got there ahead of the big centre half. *Goal!* One of the coaches was refereeing the game, and as I jogged back to the centre circle he gave me a grin and said, "You'll do for me, son!"

I was chuffed but I tried not to show it and just shrugged.

"Thanks, sir."

Was that the right thing to say? Is a football coach like one of your teachers at school? Anyway, the game carried on until there were about twenty minutes to go: and it was still 2–2.

I peered over towards the stand and I could see Dad but no sign of Jerry. Now was the time! I went up to the ref and told him I really needed the loo. "Go on, then, son," he said. "But don't take all day." I sprinted off to the changing rooms and, just as we'd planned, Jerry was there waiting for me. I got out of my kit and he put it on. I slipped into the tracksuit he'd been wearing. As quick as I'd run in, Jerry ran out. The ref waved at him, thinking it was me, and told him to come on. I sneaked out of the changing room and up into the stand. I slid into the seat behind Dad, who was so involved with the game he didn't even turn round.

I'd had my chance and now Jerry had his. I don't know what I thought might happen but I just wanted Jerry to get a taste of the big time. If worst came to worst, we'd just change clothes back again after the game. But, within a minute or two, I could see Jerry wasn't going to be satisfied with that. Other players were starting to tire but he was racing around: a man on a mission. One minute he was clearing the ball in his own six-yard box, the next, he was making a run in behind the other team's back four.

And then it happened. I knew Jerry was a good player but maybe even I didn't know *how* good. He picked up the ball just inside his own half and raced off across the pitch. Their midfielders didn't know

whether to tackle him, or stand off. He found himself out on the right, with two defenders in front of him. What did he do? He just chipped the ball over their heads and dashed between them before they could react. I held my breath. Jerry was in on goal, then as the goalie came out to close down he bent the ball around him with his left foot and it went in off the far post: you could hear the "ping" before it settled into the net.

There was a moment of complete silence, on and off the pitch. I mean, that was the kind of goal people expected to see Lionel Messi score. Jerry just clenched his fist and then ran back for kick-off as if it was something he did most days. I leapt up and gave Dad a big hug from behind.

"What about that, Dad?"

What happened next was straight out of a Tom and Jerry cartoon. Dad looked at me. Then looked out onto the pitch. Then back at me. And then, very slowly, back towards Jerry. His mouth was opening and closing like a goldfish's. Until he swung round and spluttered, "Which one *are* you?"

A few minutes later, the full-time whistle went. Rather than face Dad, I jumped out of my seat and ran down towards the pitch. I could see that the coach who'd been refereeing the game had already gone up and started talking to Jerry. I ran on, not wanting my brother to get into trouble – or, at least, not get into trouble on his own. I could hear him asking Jerry what his name was, and how old he was. Just as I got alongside them, the coach turned to me and growled, "Stay right where you are." I froze on the spot.

Then he turned back to Jerry. As the coach spoke, Jerry's eyes opened wider and wider. It turned out that Shelby Town were starting an under-11s group in a month's time. The coach wanted to talk to Dad about getting Jerry back for those trials.

"Not that I need a second look, really," he said with a grin.

His smile disappeared, though, as he turned back to me. For a minute, I thought he was going to explode. Suddenly, I wanted Dad to be there, just in case. The coach sent Jerry away and took a deep breath. "You're Tom, aren't you?"

I just nodded.

"Well, Tom. I've had boys pull some tricks on me in my time. But what I've just seen is right up there with the best of them. The worst of them, I mean. Swapping places with your brother in the middle of a match? What were you thinking?"

I just shrugged.

"Did you think I wouldn't notice? Well, I didn't at first, to be honest. It wasn't till after your brother scored that I got a good look at him. But I was bound to find out. And what did you think I'd do then?"

I just looked at the floor.

"I should be sending you on your way now, telling you that you've missed your big chance. But, right now, I'm not sure that'd be the best thing to do. What you did was wrong but, somehow, it seems to me like it was right, as well. We've had brothers together at Shelby before, but I don't think I've ever come across one who'd do what you did. You really wanted to give him a chance. And because of that, *you're* going to get a second chance."

I just grinned.

"Your brother can join the under-11s when we get them started. And you can join the under-12s from this time next week."

At that moment, Dad arrived. I was still grinning, still speechless. I ran off to tell Jerry what the coach had said. As I went, I could hear him talking to Dad.

"Ah, you're Mr Barlow, aren't you? I'm Dan Farley, one of the coaches here at Town. I think you and I need to have a chat about those boys..."

MAESTRO

(Jean-Pierre Vert's poem)

Elegant and long of limb
Midfield maestro – built to win
I'm the one who pulls the strings
See my name upon my shirt
Only one Jean-Pierre Vert

Fleet of foot and smooth and slick
I know each and every trick
I'm the one who makes them tick
Wide awake, always alert
Only one Jean-Pierre Vert

Cool and calm when heads are hot
Not a man to lose the plot
I'm the one who calls the shots
I take the pain, the strain, the hurt
Only one Jean-Pierre Vert

Taking every knock and niggle
Orchestrating from the middle
Never one for second fiddle
Conducting in the mud and dirt
Only one Jean-Pierre Vert

LETTING GO

NICK HORNBY

Jamie knew why the boss wanted to see them. The other two, Jack and Jermaine, knew too. Jamie could see it in their eyes. But none of them said anything. It was as if, just by keeping quiet, they could maybe stop it happening.

As they walked down the corridor to the manager's office at the training ground, Jamie started thinking about *The X Factor*. That bit before boot camp, when all the contestants are put into different rooms. Some rooms contain people who are going through to the next round, and some are full of people who are going to be sent home. Well, you must know which of the two you're in, mustn't you? If you look around and see some of the really good singers – the ones that the judges say have a chance of winning – then you're OK, aren't you? But if you're in a room with some croaky old granny, or a guy who weighs a hundred and fifty kilos and has a beard down to the floor, you're in trouble.

Jack and Jermaine were like two croaky old grannies. Not that they looked like croaky old grannies, of course. They were tall, muscular eighteen-year-olds. But when it came to football, and a future at Shelby Town FC, they might as well have been in their nineties. Jack was as talented as any young player at the club, but he was always in trouble. He'd been late for training loads of times, and once, when he'd been subbed with thirty minutes to go, he'd kicked a water bottle, hard, at the coach. It hadn't hit him, but it hadn't missed by much. And everyone knew he spent his Saturday nights in bars and clubs, partying with people in their twenties and thirties who thought it was cool to get a young Shelby player drunk.

Jermaine, on the other hand, was a nice kid, he just wasn't getting any better. He was getting slower, though. Or at least that's what it looked like, because over the last couple of years everyone else had got quicker. He was a left back, and in the last few games he'd been murdered by whoever he'd been up against. In the game against Charlton, the right-winger he'd been marking had scored twice and set up a third. Jermaine did everything he possibly could to work on his pace – he trained hard and did endless sprints with a fitness coach. But nothing worked. He was who he was, and he had what he'd been given, and it wasn't enough. It wasn't enough for Shelby Town, anyway.

So why was Jamie walking down the corridor with these two? What was he doing with bad boy Jack and Jermaine the Snail? He wasn't sure he could put it into words. He had technical ability, he had stamina, he had tricks; he understood football, and he had enough pace for his position in central midfield. But games just seemed to pass him by. He was always on the edge of them, never in the middle. He was in the middle of the pitch, but he wasn't in the middle of the match. He began every match thinking, This is the one. This is the one where everyone will notice me. But twenty minutes later, he knew it had happened again, that he'd somehow found himself pushed out of it. And then he found his concentration wandering, and his spirits falling. He had never told anyone this, but recently he'd spent half the games panicking and the other half thinking about life after Shelby Town.

Jermaine knocked on the office door. The three of them still weren't looking at each other. They heard a phone call finishing, and then Mick Diamond opened the door and ushered them inside. He looked serious, as if he was about to tell them that someone had died. Jamie was relieved to realize that it didn't feel like that to him.

There were three chairs lined up ready for them, and they sat down without being invited. Diamond returned to his seat behind the desk.

"I'm not going to drag this out," he said. "We're letting you go."

Nobody said anything. There wasn't anything to say. Jamie gave the other two a sidelong glance and could see that Jermaine was trying hard not to cry.

"I'm sorry," the manager went on. "We like to think that we look after our young players here, and we'll give you as much help as possible with finding a new club. We'll sit down with you individually and talk to you about what you want to do. We can make introductions and recommendations, and with a bit of luck you still have a future in the game. We always involve your parents in any—"

Suddenly, Jack stood up and kicked his chair over. It happened so quickly that it made Jamie jump. Then Jack swore, walked out and slammed the door. Jamie never saw him again. He heard months later that Jack was in Portugal, playing for some Second Division team. But when Jamie tried Googling his name, the only links he got were to the Shelby Town website.

Mick Diamond shrugged. "That doesn't make me feel like we're making the wrong decision," he said.

Jamie had a nice car. It was one of the only things he'd spent proper cash on since he'd started at Shelby. He still had a bit of money in the bank. Maybe it was because he knew he wasn't ever going to make big money from the game: Wayne Rooney money. Maybe that's what separated the great players from the OK ones. The ones who went on to make it never doubted they would make it. Was it only the doubt that stopped him from being great? Or was he doubtful because he wasn't any good? What came first, the chicken or the egg? He'd never know.

He drove home slowly, radio on loud. He was more worried about talking to his dad than he had been about talking to Diamond. Unlike just about everyone else in the team, Jamie had grown up in Shelby. His dad was a season-ticket holder, a Town fan all his life. The last few years, he'd started to dream about watching his son lift the Premier League trophy, or lead the team out at a European final, or score the winning goal in a big game at Manor Park.

Jamie waited until they were eating their dinner. "They're not giving me a new contract, Dad," he said quietly.

"'Course they are," said his dad. "You're their best player."

Jamie stared at him.

"Are there any more potatoes, Karen?" his dad asked. His mum looked at Jamie. She understood. His dad carried on chomping his way through his dinner as if Jamie had just told him he was going out to the cinema.

"Did you hear me?" Jamie said.

"I'm not deaf. I'm just telling you, they will."

"I was called in to Mick Diamond's office this afternoon. With Jermaine and Jack. He offered to help us find new clubs."

Finally, his dad got it. He stopped chewing, and stared at his plate for a long time.

"Did Diamond tell you why?"

"No."

"Didn't you ask him?"

"No. I knew why."

"So you just sat there and accepted it?"

"What was I supposed to do? Argue with him?"

"Show him you care. Show him you want it!"

"It's not about wanting it, Dad. It's about not being good enough."

"That's your trouble, right there," said his father. "You just give up. No fight."

His mum put down her knife and fork. "Stop it, David," she said. "Leave him alone. This is his disappointment, not yours."

But that wasn't really true, Jamie saw suddenly. The disappointment was all his father's.

The next day, Derek Hardaker from the Academy took him to one side before training. "There's a lot of interest in both you and Jermaine," he told him.

"That was quick," said Jamie. Hardaker looked a bit sheepish, and Jamie felt stupid. Of course, they'd been letting other clubs know for a while that he was being let go.

"Orient are interested," he went on. "And Lincoln City are desperate. They'd offer you a contract today if you wanted one. Good little club, Lincoln. Well run.

And a nice place to live, too."

"Can I think about it?" Jamie asked.

"You should be telling them that, not me. Talk to them first. Go and have a look around."

"I don't know."

"Don't hang around waiting for Manchester United to come calling, son." Mr Hardaker wasn't being unkind. He put an arm on Jamie's shoulder to prove it.

"I'm not," said Jamie. "I don't know if I want to stay in the game, that's all."

"Really?"

Jamie looked at the Academy Director. "You sound surprised."

"Sorry," Hardaker said. "I just didn't – well, I didn't know you were interested in anything else, that's all."

Something else he didn't know was that with those words Derek Hardaker made Jamie's mind up for him.

That was then, two years ago, but this is now. Jamie is preparing to take a free kick, right-footed, ten metres outside the penalty area. He fancies trying to bend it into the top corner, but there are only a couple of minutes to go, and it's a cup tie, and the score is 1–1. If he gets it wrong, he knows he'll get slaughtered by the rest of the team. So he whips it in, with pace, and at a decent height, and it's the right decision.

Danny Collister gets his head to it and puts it right into the bottom corner.

Danny runs over to the touchline with his shirt over his head. There's no crowd, but there are people watching. Danny is on the same course as Jamie, and half a dozen of their classmates are standing in a huddle, cheering and laughing, as Danny slides on his stomach in the mud.

Jamie loves playing for North Shelby College. It helps that the team is top of the league, and if they hang on here they'll be into the cup semi-final. But what Jamie loves most is knowing that he can control the game. The truth is, he's better than everyone else, teammates and opponents. He's not miles better, but good enough. He's never out of his depth, and he never loses concentration or panics, like he used to when he played for Shelby under-18s. And he's not out of his depth in his lectures, either. He passed Level 1 of the NVQ in Sports and Recreation without too much trouble, and he's enjoying Level 2. At Shelby Town, he realizes now, he'd spent every day waiting to be told that he'd failed.

In the final couple of minutes, they have to defend a corner, but it doesn't make it over the head of the first defender. When the ball is thumped clear, the ref blows the whistle.

As Jamie is coming off the pitch, he sees a guy wearing a dark puffa jacket and a baseball cap walk towards him quickly. Jamie has spent a lot of time in his life with men like this, and doesn't really want to spend any more.

"Jamie, son, can I have a quick word?"

"I really want to get changed and go home," says Jamie.

"I know it didn't work out for you at Shelby," says the man, "but you're wasted on this lot. I've been watching you the last few games, and I think you should come down to—"

"I'm sorry," Jamie interrupts. "I'm not interested."

"You don't even know what I was going to say."

"It doesn't matter," says Jamie. "But thanks anyway." And he jogs after his teammates towards the college changing rooms.

(Peter Ball's poem)

I'm Peter – got my eye on the ball
Never left and always back
I will stave off your attack
Keep my teammates right on track
Left back Peter Ball

I'm Peter – got my eye on the ball
No winger leaves me for dead
No one blue, white or red
I will get the ball instead
Left back Peter Ball

I'm Peter – got my eye on the ball
Timing tackles to perfection
Anticipating each deflection
I'm the natural selection
Left back Peter Ball

DECISIONS, DECISIONS

ALAN SEFTON

Stuart Dolan was pacing up and down outside the Academy Director's office. That tight, narrow corridor with no windows. No wonder he felt trapped. But he'd had a message that Mr Hardaker wanted to see him, so he'd changed as quickly as he could after training and got over to the administration block.

③

HARDAKER

He didn't know what Mr Hardaker wanted. And Mr Hardaker didn't know that Stuart actually wanted to see him anyway. There was something playing on his mind. Not a personal problem exactly: Stuart wouldn't have felt like discussing that sort of thing with Shelby Town's Academy Director. But this was nagging away at him and he knew he should have mentioned it ages ago.

Through the thin door of the office, Stuart could hear Mr Hardaker speaking to someone on the phone. He couldn't make out what the conversation was about. He'd just hear Mr Hardaker speak, then silence. Then Mr Hardaker speaking again. The longer Stuart waited, the edgier he became. He already had one problem on his mind. Now he might have another: what did Mr Hardaker want him for? Had he done something wrong?

As his teammates walked past him on their way down to the canteen, squeezing by in the narrow corridor, Stuart's long wait turned into a procession of banter and backchat. They all deliberately bumped into him and then made what they thought were hilarious comments about how much trouble he was in.

What made things worse was that waiting in the corridor brought back bad memories for Stuart. Only a couple of weeks ago, his headmaster at school had called him to his office and kept him waiting outside for what seemed like hours. Teachers had been complaining about his behaviour in class and about him not keeping up with his homework. The headmaster told Stuart that the school felt he was only thinking about football. If things didn't improve, the head threatened to stop him joining Shelby Town's Youth Academy. Without the school's permission, Stuart knew, he wouldn't be able to realize his dream of signing for the club.

Now, waiting for the Academy Director, Stuart put his ear to the door. Mr Hardaker was still talking, so he decided to get a breath of fresh air to clear his head. On the first pitch outside, the reserve team squad was playing a small-sided game. But Stuart was too nervous to watch and soon made his way back into the office block.

He put his ear to Mr Hardaker's door again. Silence. Stuart took a deep breath and knocked on the door. No answer. He knocked again. Nothing. He tried the handle. It wouldn't budge; the door was locked. How long had he been away, watching the reserves? A minute or two? Maybe five? Long enough to miss Mr Hardaker, who, it seemed, had packed up and gone.

Nervous before, Stuart was miserable – and worried – now. He checked with reception and the lady told him

Mr Hardaker had just left and said he wouldn't be back for the rest of the day. Almost in a daze, a blizzard of thoughts rushing through his mind, Stuart headed for the bus stop and home.

When he got in, he barely said a word to his mum, gulped down his tea and rushed back out of the house. Whenever Stuart was bothered about something, whenever he needed someone to talk to or someone to ask for advice, he knew where to go. The one person he could turn to. The one person he could rely on: his granddad.

"Granddad, I need to talk to you about something at Shelby. Mr Hardaker – you know, the Academy Director – wants to see me. I'm terrified. Whenever anyone's called to his office, it's never good news. I went along this afternoon and I was only away for a minute but I missed him."

Granddad puffed out his cheeks and tried to look Stuart in the eye. "Slow down, son. I can't keep up with you."

Stuart gulped in some air. "Well, you see, it could be the same thing I've been meaning to speak to *him* about. I should've said something ages ago but I just couldn't pluck up the courage."

"And what's that, Stuart?"

"The Leeside Cup."

"What about it?"

Stuart didn't really know where to start so he plunged straight in. "Well, when you join an academy, you can only play non-academy games with permission from the Director. You know, games for any team other than the club. It's an FA rule. They're really strict about the number of games boys can play during a season. It's something to do with them not wanting young players to risk getting injuries by playing too many matches."

Granddad nodded. "Sounds fair enough."

"Yeah, but the Leeside Cup in Year Eleven is the biggest competition in schools' football around here. Everyone wants to play in it; every school wants to win it. Until I joined the Academy at Shelby Town, I always played for the school, played with my mates. Then, all of a sudden, I had to stop playing with them. Some of my friends thought I'd got too big for my boots because I'd signed for Shelby. It was terrible."

Granddad could see from Stuart's face how much that upset him, but he didn't say anything, just nodded and let Stuart carry on.

"And it wasn't just that. There was all the other stuff I couldn't do with them any more either: no late-night chats on the phone or Facebook; no Friday-night parties; even the cinema finished too late for me. McDonald's was out of bounds as well. At Shelby they tell you that, even though you're young, you should give yourself the best chance; and that means living like a professional player."

Granddad smiled. "Well, you'll have plenty of time for junk food and rubbish films when you're older, won't you?"

"'Course. The one thing I know for sure is that I want to play for Shelby Town. But there's the Leeside Cup. I started thinking about it. Wouldn't that be one way I could show my mates how much playing with them still meant to me? Especially if we could go and win the biggest trophy of the lot."

Stuart suddenly stopped talking. Granddad looked at him. "Well?"

There was a nervous silence. "So I decided to play for the school. And I didn't tell anyone that I wasn't meant to. And I didn't dare ask Mr Hardaker about it because I was worried he'd say no. We've got to the semi-finals, though, Granddad. And the club's bound to find out, aren't they?"

Granddad didn't want to say the first thing that

came into his head and he certainly didn't want to make things worse. "Tell you what – let me sleep on it. Come round in the morning, early. I'll do us a big breakfast and we can talk about it then, before you go off to school."

"What, another sleepless night?"

"Come on, Stuart. This isn't the end of the world."

"It might not seem like it to you, Granddad. But Shelby Town *is* my world and it could be the end of it when Mr Hardaker finds out what I've done."

Granddad walked to the door with his grandson, grabbed his shoulders and gave him a big hug. Stuart already looked like a young man but Granddad knew he was still a boy in lots of ways. "See you in the morning. Get yourself a good night's sleep. And come round here as early as you want."

Stuart pushed his plate across the table.

"More bacon?" asked Granddad.

"No thanks, I'm stuffed."

Granddad grinned. "Amazing isn't it? A proper breakfast can take your mind off almost anything. You need to get yourself off to school. And then, this afternoon, first chance you get, you've got to tell Mr Hardaker about the Leeside Cup. Or you do if you want to carry on playing for the school in the competition, anyway. Like you said, he's bound to find out. From the semi-finals onwards, the Cup gets a big spread in the local paper. They preview the games and then carry proper match reports; interviews and photos, the lot. So you can't exactly play under a different name or in disguise, especially when you'll be scoring all the goals!"

Granddad paused. Stuart looked at him, mouth wide open. As always, Granddad was telling Stuart what he really thought, not just what he thought Stuart wanted to hear. "You've got to be honest with him, son. Tell him exactly what you told me. And do it today! You were wrong to leave it so long. You already know that. And the longer you put off dealing with a problem, the worse it becomes."

Stuart was already on his way out the door and up the road before his granddad could say any more. He didn't need to be late for school on top of everything else. He just about heard Granddad call after him, "And don't forget to come round and tell me what happens."

Stuart had barely taken a step into Mr Hardaker's office. "Stuart!" boomed the Academy Director, furious. "Why didn't you come and see me yesterday?" Before

Stuart could even open his mouth to reply, Mr Hardaker continued even more angrily. "Straight after training, I want to see you back here in my office!"

Training didn't go well. Stuart mis-hit passes, misjudged crosses and shinned any number of shots. Watching him, you might have wondered what he was doing at the Academy in the first place. But Stuart had other things on his mind. Were the coaches aware of that? Certainly nobody gave him a bad time, just words of encouragement. But they passed Stuart by. All he could think about was the meeting he had to go to at the end of the session.

By the time he'd had a quick shower and got changed, he'd worked out a plan. He walked down the corridor where he'd sweated away an hour the previous afternoon. This time, when he arrived at Mr Hardaker's office, he didn't listen at the door to find out whether the Director was busy on the phone. He knocked, walked straight in and started talking without even waiting to be asked.

"Mr Hardaker, I'm sorry I missed you yesterday. There was a misunderstanding but it was probably my fault. Anyway, I know you've asked me to come here so you can tell me off about the Leeside Cup. I know I've handled the situation badly but I hope you'll give me a chance to explain."

Mr Hardaker gave a little cough. He wanted to interrupt Stuart but there was no stopping him, he was already in full flow.

"I know I'm not meant to play for any other team without asking you first. I'd been meaning to come and see you but I just couldn't face it. I was scared, really. But once we reached the semi-finals – I mean the school reached the semi-finals – I knew I had to talk it over with you. Tell you what I'd done. You know, before you read about it in the local paper. And then you called me in to see you, which is when I started getting *really* worried."

Mr Hardaker looked down at some papers on his desk. Then he looked up at Stuart with a stern expression.

"Stuart, do you really think I don't know you've been playing in the Leeside Cup? Don't you realize that it's my job to know everything there is to know about local youth football? In fact, I've seen all your games right from the start of the competition."

Stuart was dumbfounded. Mr Hardaker looked at his player's face, eyes wide with astonishment, and smiled.

"S-so you knew all along?" stammered Stuart.

Mr Hardaker was still smiling.

"And you don't mind?" asked Stuart.

"Hm, I didn't say that exactly. But I like Academy boys to be independent, to think for themselves and make their own decisions. You have to make your own decisions on the pitch. And in the rest of your life, too, for that matter. But why didn't you come and discuss it with me?"

"I thought you'd say no and then I'd have to let my school down. And my mates. To be honest, I really miss not playing with them any more."

Mr Hardaker nodded, as if he was trying hard to understand Stuart's point of view.

"Fair enough. I understand the situation. And, to be honest, I don't think I need to interfere one way or the other. I think it's your decision. You just should have come to see me right at the start."

Suddenly, Stuart felt as if a huge weight had been lifted from his shoulders. He slumped down in the nearest chair to get his breath back. But then a new thought dawned on him. "But, Mr Hardaker, if it wasn't the Leeside Cup you wanted to see me about, what was it?"

Mr Hardaker stood up and crossed the room. He held out his hand. And a letter. "Congratulations, Stuart. You'd better take this home for your parents to have a look at. You've been called up to train with the England squad for the youth international in two weeks' time."

Stuart felt as if somebody had just punched him very hard in the stomach. He started to tremble, almost as if he was going to burst into tears. And when he tried to speak, all that came out was a little squeak.

"What's the matter?" asked a confused Mr Hardaker.

Stuart looked down at the letter and scanned it quickly for what he needed to see. When he found the date for his England call-up, all the colour drained from his face and he slumped back in his chair.

"But this is the same day as the Leeside Cup semi-final!"

Trials &
Tribulations

CURTIS DAVIES

34 Carlton Way
Epsley Farm
Dodsworth
Herts

Dear Auntie Ruby,

Thanks for the letter for my birthday. And thanks for the
£30. I'm not going to spend it on football boots, though, like
you said. I had some bad news this week. You know I've been
training with Watford for five years now, since I was eleven.
They rang me yesterday to say that they weren't going to
offer me a place for next year. I've had great coaching there
but the thing is, they had to make a decision about numbers
and they didn't think they had room for me. They said they'd
give me a reference for football or anything in the future.

Mum wasn't happy. She thinks it's because the club didn't
like me putting my schoolwork first. I had to miss a couple
of games last season because of my GCSEs. There were a

couple of other boys in the same situation as me, though, and they got offered places by the club, so I don't think that's the reason. Plus Watford always said they supported me doing my exams, and I believe them.

So what am I going to do? Well, I spoke to one of the coaches at Watford, Vic, and to my PE teacher at St Mark's, Mr Holden. They both said that it would be worth me contacting other clubs to see if I could get a trial. So I'm spending my birthday money on a new pen and paper, some envelopes and about thirty first-class stamps. Then I'll save up my money from the summer job at Shelton's to get those new boots!

Love you, Auntie. Hope we'll see you soon.

Marky

Shelby Town FC
Manor Park
Balcom Drive
Shelby
Leeside

Dear Mr Hardaker,

My name is Mark Bing. I'm sixteen. I'm left-footed and generally play centre half or defensive midfield, but I have also played fullback. I have been training with Watford Football Club for the past five years but have been told that they will not be offering me a place as an Academy scholar next season. I am writing to ask if it would be possible to come along to have a trial for Shelby Town in the next few weeks. Here are some details about myself:

Name:	Mark Bing
Nationality:	English
Address:	34 Carlton Way, Epsley Farm, Dodsworth, Herts
DOB:	14/3/96
Height:	180 cm
Weight:	73 kg
Position:	Centre half/defensive midfield

Playing history:

School teams:	Farringdon Primary, Dodsworth
	St Mark's, Dodsworth (Captain, Ist XI)

Representative:	Played for Mid-Herts in Inter-District Championships
	Played for Herts County under-14s and under-15s
Club teams:	Tenby Juniors, Sappington (under-10s and under-14s), playing in the Mid-Herts Minor Rural League
Pro club:	Under-11s trials at Tottenham Hotspur, Milton Keynes Dons and Wycombe Wanderers; joined Watford at under-11s

I started out as a left back, but in the under-14s, the staff at Watford moved me to centre back. Last year I was tried out as a defensive midfielder and felt comfortable there. I think my strengths as a player are that I am quick, a good header of the ball and comfortable in possession. The coaching staff at Watford told my parents that they were very happy with my attitude in training and in games.

References:

Mr Michael Holden: Head of Sport, St Mark's Secondary School, Dodsworth

Mr Vic Murray: Youth Team Coach, Watford FC, Vicarage Road, Watford

I hope that you will give me a chance to show what I can do. I am currently waiting for my GCSE results (I sat eight subjects) and have a part-time job on the customer services desk at Shelton's in Dodsworth. I can get up to Shelby Town to meet you any time.

I hope to hear from you soon.
Yours sincerely,

Mark Bing

Shelby Town FC
Manor Park • Balcom Drive
Shelby • Leeside

Dear Mark,

Thanks for your letter. We are always on the lookout for young players at Shelby Town and I am happy to see you either next Thursday evening (23rd) or the following (30th) for a trial. I know Vic Holden at Watford and he speaks very highly of you. Our youth team coach, Graham Hicks, remembers you playing against our under-15s last season. We can't make any sort of commitment at this stage, of course, but we would like to see how you train with next season's scholars.

Perhaps you or your parents would like to telephone my secretary, Marjorie North, on the Shelby Town club number to make the arrangements. We would like you to come to Manor Park for around 6.30 p.m. and we will arrange transport from there to the training ground, where you'll be met by Graham. We will also supply you with training kit for use on the night, so just bring your boots and shin pads! Look forward to seeing you, Mark.

Best regards,

Derek Hardaker
Academy Director
Shelby Town FC

34 Carlton Way
Epsley Farm
Dodsworth
Herts

Dear Mrs Violett,

I am just writing to say that I will not be able to do my shift at the store next Thursday night (30th) because I have been asked to go for a trial at Shelby Town FC. I will let you know how I get on and how this will affect my work for the rest of the summer. Thank you for being so understanding about the situation.

Yours sincerely,

Mark Bing

Shelton's
Supermarket

Customer Services
Shelton's Supermarket
Jarrett Road
Dodsworth

Dear Mark,

Thanks for your letter. Very nice and old-fashioned. Makes a change from a phone call or a text message! That's fine about next week. Terry Dore will be able to cover you. Good luck with the trial. Fingers crossed for you!

Best wishes,

Audrey Violett

34 Carlton Way
Epsley Farm
Dodsworth
Herts

Dear Auntie Ruby,

Sorry if my writing looks a bit wobbly. I am on the train, on my way up to Shelby for training again. I went for that trial last week and it all went really well. I was nervous when I got there but when I walked into the ground the first person I saw was Niall Trotman. I don't know if you remember him. Niall and me went to primary school together and he came out to St Lucia with us once when we were kids. His mum has family on the island as well, up in Castries. Anyway, we had lost touch, but there he was at Shelby Town for a trial just like me! Small world.

Well, the trial was good — just training and fitness stuff and then small-sided games. I felt pretty good once we got started. It must have gone OK because they said they want me to come up every Tuesday and Thursday for the next six weeks. Colchester was the only other club that offered me a trial, but I think it's best to just try to get on at Shelby Town for now.

The only problem is getting up there! The way the trains are, I have to get one into London and then one back out to Shelby, which means it costs quite a lot in fares and takes ages. We get finished about ten and I'm not home till about half past eleven. Mad. But it's worth it. So, sorry if the writing's not the best to read. Talk to you soon.

Love you, Auntie.

Marky

Blue Flash Couriers
Head Office
43 St John Street
London EC1

Dear Mr Bing,

I am writing to confirm what we discussed at the meeting at the Dodsworth depot earlier this month. Unfortunately, these are difficult economic times and we are going to have to close the Dodsworth depot with immediate effect. This means we will be letting you go at the end of this week. You will, of course, be paid up to date and I will bear you in mind, should any work arise at one of our London branches. However, it is unlikely that it will as we have had to review all our operations in view of the downturn in business over the past year.

I would like to thank you for your hard work as a driver for Blue Flash Couriers. Everyone at the company wishes you the very best of luck for the future.

Kind regards,

Anthony Holmes
Managing Director
Blue Flash Couriers

34 Carlton Way
Epsley Farm
Dodsworth
Herts

Dear Mr Hardaker,

I am writing to explain that things have changed for me and my family so I'm no longer able to train at Manor Park. My dad was made redundant last week, which means we are going to have to be more careful about money. Also, now that I have started coming up for games at Shelby Town on Saturday mornings, I have had to give up my part-time job.

I have really enjoyed my time at Shelby Town. Thank you very much for offering me a trial. I know you haven't yet made any decisions about which boys to keep on for the new season. But in the meantime I plan to find a local Sunday league team to play for, and I will look for another part-time job while I do my A levels. I think I told you that I got my GCSE results and passed seven subjects, so I will carry on at St Mark's. I hope you will understand.

Yours sincerely,

Mark Bing

Shelby Town FC
Manor Park • Balcom Drive
Shelby • Leeside

Dear Mark,

Thanks for your letter. You are right that we haven't yet made decisions about our triallists but we would be sorry to see you lose touch with Shelby Town. We have enjoyed having you with us. I am writing to say that we would be happy to cover all your expenses by way of train fares, etc., if you would like to continue training at Manor Park for the time being. We will be making final decisions about scholars in the next month or so.

Let me know what you would like to do.

Best regards,

Derek Hardaker

Academy Director
Shelby Town FC

34 Carlton Way
Epsley Farm
Dodsworth
Herts

Dear Auntie Ruby,

Hope everything's good there. Wouldn't mind a few days on the beach myself! I overheard you on the phone to Mum the other night. It would be great if you were over for Christmas this year. Dad losing his job was bad news but he's doing mini-cab work around Watford and then he's going to see about getting something as a chauffeur. The guy at Blue Arrow said he might have a couple of people for Dad to try.

Anyway, I know Mum told you that Shelby Town are helping out with train fares and everything, so I'm still training up there three times a week. I'm still waiting to find out whether they're going to pick me for next season. I think I've been doing OK. The last few days, though, my ankle's been really sore. I fell down the step in the back garden last week and it still hurts when I try to run and turn. But I can't tell Shelby Town that. All the lads would just laugh at me for getting injured in the garden! I said something to Niall about it and he brought a walking stick to training the next night. You remember what he's like for taking the mickey. I'm going to see the doctor about it tomorrow.

Love you, Auntie.

Marky

WILBERFORCE SURGERY

72 Ansett Way
Epsley Farm
Dodsworth

Dear Mark Bing,

As requested, I am writing to confirm my medical assessment of your ankle. I do not believe that you have sustained a serious injury. However, I would advise that you rest your ankle for a week. I do not think it would be a good idea to risk playing competitive sport. I am enclosing some information from our practice nurse, which includes some rehabilitation exercises that you may find useful.

Yours faithfully,

Dr Roger Clark

Shelby Town FC
Manor Park • Balcom Drive
Shelby • Leeside

Dear Mark,

Thanks for sending on the letter from your doctor. I must say, we were a little surprised that you didn't speak to us about this earlier. We would have been happy to ask our club doctor to look at your ankle.

Can I suggest that you attend training as usual this Thursday evening and I will ask our reserve team physio to have a look at the injury then?

Let me know by phone, please, whether or not you can be at Manor Park for 6 p.m. on Thursday.

Regards,

Derek Hardaker

Academy Director
Shelby Town FC

34 Carlton Way
Epsley Farm
Dodsworth
Herts

Dear Mr Hicks,

I have just got home from training and I am still upset about what happened tonight. I appreciate all the coaching and advice you have given me the past few weeks. But, with all due respect, I do not think that as team coach it is up to you to say whether or not my ankle is anything to worry about, especially when two of the Shelby first team squad were in the physio's room at the time. I also can't believe you suggested that if I was serious about my football I wouldn't be moaning about my ankle and would just get on and play.

I want you to know that football is the most important thing in my life and I take it very seriously indeed. But not enough to put up with somebody shouting at me when I haven't done anything wrong. I only went to my GP so as not to bother anybody at Shelby Town.

I am not sorry that I was worried about my ankle, but I am sorry that I shouted back at you. I am old enough to know better. Anyway, if you want me to stop coming to training at Shelby Town, I will understand.

Yours sincerely,

Mark Bing

Shelby Town FC
Manor Park • Balcom Drive
Shelby • Leeside

Dear Triallist,

We will be making our decisions about next season after a game at the Bescot Stadium against a Walsall XI team on Saturday week. We will be travelling from Manor Park by coach, departing at 10 a.m. for a 2 p.m. kick-off. We should be back in Shelby by about 7.30 p.m. Please let me know in advance if you have family or friends who wish to make their way to the Bescot Stadium for the game. Walsall FC have very kindly offered to provide refreshments but need an idea of numbers. In the meantime, training continues as usual on Tuesday and Thursday evenings.

Regards,

Derek Hardaker

Academy Director
Shelby Town FC

Piton Cottage
Sir Arthur Lewis Street
Soufrière
St Lucia

Marky!

Hope everything is OK with you. I've had your mum on the phone a couple of times this week about your argument with this coach at the football club. I expect you know that. She said you were pretty upset.

Well, two things. First, you have to look after yourself, Mark. You know whether you are fit enough to play or to train and you have your future to consider. You must only listen to the doctor.

Second, you are just like your dad in so many ways. Most of them good, before you go asking me! What I mean is that your dad always knows when to stick up for himself too. You were right to say what you did. I know you are only sixteen, even though you are six feet tall and look like a grown man! It's right that you don't let this guy push you around or bully you.

Now, Mum said that they have written to you about a game when they'll decide on next season's players. I don't know what you are going to do – if you will go or not, or whether you have already finished with them because of the argument you had. Like I say, whatever happens, whatever you decide, I am proud of you. It will be for the best. After all, there are other football clubs than Shelby Town, aren't there?

Let me know how you get on when you have a chance.

Till then, love you, Marky.

Auntie Ruby

34 Carlton Way
Epsley Farm
Dodsworth
Herts

Dear Auntie Ruby,

I got your letter and I'm writing straight back. First of all, I should tell you that the coach at Shelby, Mr Hicks, is not a bully. He has been very positive and helpful towards me since I began training there. I think that's why I was so angry when he had a go at me. It wasn't like him at all. I wrote to him about it but he hasn't written back.

Anyhow, I went to training last night and I've decided to stay and see what happens. I'm not sure they will want me to stay anyway. Not because of the argument but because they've had a boy come down from Newcastle United. He's been released from there and his family are living in Aylesbury now. From what I saw in training, it looks like they really like him and he's a left-footed centre half just like me. I was put in midfield and at left back in the practice games this week.

Still, at least my ankle is feeling OK now. Thanks for sticking up for me, Auntie. Lucky for Mr Hicks that you're far away and can't go and tell him what you think! Boy, would he think twice then!

I will let you know how I get on this week and we'll see what happens up at Walsall.

Love you, Auntie.

Marky

Shelby Town FC
Manor Park • Balcom Drive
Shelby • Leeside

SHELBY TOWN FC, MANOR PARK, LEESIDE

FAO ALL TRIALLISTS:

TEAM TO PLAY WALSALL XI

KO SATURDAY 2 p.m., BESCOT STADIUM

TEAM:	SUBS:
HAMPTON (GK)	CUMMINGS (GK)
SHARP, A	WILLIAMSON
ROBERTS	SALMON
EFFIONG	VALENTINE
OLIVEIRA	SHARP, D
MARRIOTT	BING
FINDLAY	
TROTMAN	
LAMBROU	
SIMMONS	
ADEYEMI	

34 Carlton Way
Epsley Farm
Dodsworth
Herts

Dear Auntie Ruby,

Oh! What a day! Can you imagine how I felt when
I looked at the team sheet for that game at Walsall?
My big chance — maybe my only chance — before
Shelby Town decided which triallists they were going
to take on for the next couple of years. I looked down
the eleven names and mine wasn't there.

Ben Roberts, the lad from Newcastle, was in at centre
half. Me? I was the very last name on the list of subs.
It seemed like such a kick in the teeth after the last
couple of months — getting all the way up to Shelby
two or three times a week, packing in my job at the
supermarket, working as hard as I could. And the
morning of the game it felt like they were taking me
along just to make up the numbers.

I almost turned round and went straight home. Maybe
I would've done if Niall hadn't said I should be there just
in case. He more or less pushed me onto the minibus, to
be honest. I hardly said a word to him or to anyone else
on the way to the stadium. I was glad Mum and Dad
wouldn't be going to the game. They said it would have
cost quite a bit in petrol. Plus they didn't want to put
any extra pressure on me by being there.

We got to Walsall and had some sandwiches before we went out to warm up on the pitch. Such a nice day: sun shining, good pitch, a real football stadium. This was everything I'd ever wanted and it felt like it had all been taken away from me. When the boys went out to kick off, I tried to put on a brave face and wish them luck and everything. As I was shaking Ben Roberts's hand, Mr Hicks looked at me and smiled. He gave me a little thumbs up and I just couldn't work out why. I thought I'd been left out of the team because I'd had that argument with him a fortnight ago.

The game started and it soon turned out that Walsall were a really good team. A lot of their lads looked older and stronger than us. They went 2–0 up in no time at all. I felt strange, watching from the bench: in a way, I kind of wanted it to turn out like this but, at the same time, these were my mates. I didn't want them to get beaten.

At half-time, it was 4–1 to Walsall. We'd got a goal back when Lambros Lambrou scored from a corner but they'd gone up the other end and got two more almost straight away. They looked like they could score every time they attacked. When the boys came in at half-time, Mr Hicks put his arm around Ben Roberts's shoulder. Maybe Ben had had a little knock. So Mr Hicks told me to get stripped off and go on in the second half.

Suddenly, I could hardly breathe and I kept hoping nobody would see my hands shaking while I was doing up my laces! I don't really know what I was thinking.

Just: Go out and play. I'd already made up my mind that Shelby were going to let me go, so what did I have to lose? In the second half Walsall picked up where they had left off, coming at us over and over again for the first ten minutes. I don't know how they didn't score. The goalie, Greg Hampton, made a couple of fantastic saves.

An hour gone and it was still 4–1. Then maybe they got tired or we just started to feel more confident, and it seemed like we were going forwards more and more. Alec Findlay put over a corner and, as I was falling backwards at the far post, I managed to head the ball back across goal. One of Walsall's defenders put up his arm to block it and the ref pointed to the spot. Denis Adeyemi scored the penalty and we were back in the game.

Five minutes left and it was starting to seem like we'd run out of time. We were still two goals behind. But then Niall picked up the ball out on the wing and just started running. He got into the area and, because we'd already had one penalty, none of the Walsall players seemed to want to tackle him. Niall just kept going. He put the ball in through the goalie's legs. Even though we were still losing, Niall went crazy, as if he'd just scored the winning goal in a cup final!

There were just a couple of minutes to go and I'd forgotten all about the trials and about what might happen afterwards. I was just into the game, tackling as hard as I could and shouting at the other lads to get forwards. I was on the halfway line when the ball rolled to me. I don't know what came over me — I'm a centre half, remember! — but I passed to Niall and ran towards the Walsall area. Niall slipped the ball inside to me and then made a run for the box. I saw him, but I thought: *It's now or never.* I was just outside the D. I could hear Niall shouting at me because he knew what I was going to do: "No, Marky, no! Pass to me!" But I just swung my left foot and *Pow!*

Auntie! I knew as soon as I connected what was going to happen. Ninety-nine times out of a hundred that ball would have ended up in the stand but, this time, it just flew into the top corner. Their keeper dived but couldn't get near it ... 4–4, right at the end! And the next thing I knew, I was at the bottom of a pile of players. I could hear Niall laughing and shouting, "Why didn't you pass, Marky?" It was just about the best feeling I'd ever had in football.

Well, you know what happened next, don't you? In the dressing room after the match, Mr Hicks asked me if I could keep a secret. Then he said that Mr Hardaker would be writing to me offering me an Academy scholar place at Shelby Town. I just looked at him and said, "But didn't you think I wasn't serious enough about football?" He laughed and said that he'd only had a go at me to test me out. He said he did that to all the boys to see if they had the temperament to go with the talent. I didn't know what to say, so I just gave him a big hug. For once, it was Mr Hicks who didn't know what to say next!

And then, after we got changed, we came out into the car park to get on the bus. Guess who was there? Mum and Dad, of course! They said they wouldn't have missed the match for anything. I hoped Mr Hicks would understand because, even though it was supposed to be a secret, there was no way I was keeping my big news from my mum and dad.

And now you know, too, Auntie! The letter came from Mr Hardaker yesterday. He even made a joke in it about me being switched to centre forward after that goal at Walsall. We start pre-season training at Manor Park in three weeks' time. Wish me luck. I already know that the hard work starts here!

Love you,

Marky

BIG MATCH DEBUT

(Stuart Dolan's poem)

This is my moment
What I've been working for
The hours of training
Big match debut

Lining up with the big boys
Lining up against the big boys
Me – on the same pitch
Big match debut

Hoping that everything goes right
Hoping that nothing goes wrong
Hoping that I'm not embarrassed
Big match debut

Not letting the manager down
Not letting my teammates down
Not letting the fans down
Big match debut

Just one slice of luck
Just one bounce of the ball
And I could be hero or villain
On my big match debut

DEAL
OR NO DEAL?

MATT HOLLAND

MOR-GONE?
Latest from Manor Park is that Spanish side
Getafe have joined Birmingham, Sunderland
and Blackburn on the list of clubs chasing Dave
Morgan. The Shelby Town skipper, 32, is out of
contract in the summer and can talk to other
clubs in January about a big-money move that
could see him TRIPLE his wages.

Reading that made me feel weird. I might only be thirteen but I know enough about football to know that half of what you read in the papers is made up anyway. But even so. That little bit in the paper was like a little punch in the stomach. Stories about Wayne Rooney or Steven Gerrard – or even other players at Shelby Town, like Stuart Dolan or Jean-Pierre Vert – wouldn't ever bother me. Then again, my form tutor, Mrs Anderson, would never bother to cut out a story about any of those people and give it to me before assembly. But she cut out that story, that morning. Because the Dave Morgan they were writing about happens to be my dad.

I'm sure Mrs Anderson thought she was being helpful, but I can't say I agree with her. I try not to talk about Dad too much at school. I always think it's best to leave that to other people. Otherwise, I'd probably end up in a fight every Monday morning if Shelby Town had lost a game that weekend. Not knowing anything about football – or about my dad – doesn't stop people thinking they do. If they hear Alan Hansen say something on *Match of the Day*, they take it as gospel and by Monday it's as if they'd thought of it themselves.

Funnily enough, my friends aren't the problem. They either don't mention Dad or they talk to me as if they're pretending I'm not Dave Morgan's son. It's actually the teachers who go on about it. They always want to talk about the Town games and what's going on at Manor Park. And Mrs Anderson's the worst. Even though before I was put in her class she'd never been interested in football. So, while we were lining up for assembly that morning, she passed me the little square cut out from the newspaper, headlined *MOR-GONE?*, and gave me a funny look as if to say, *Mmm. What do you think about that, then?*

Well, I thought quite a lot about it, actually. In fact, I had trouble thinking about anything else. The idea of Dad changing clubs nagged away at me all day long. I might just as well have gone straight home after assembly because I definitely wasn't concentrating on any of my lessons. And there wasn't anybody at school I was going to talk to about what was on my mind. If Dad left Shelby Town, that would mean us moving house, me changing school, me leaving behind all my old friends and having to make new ones somewhere else. But I wasn't so worried about all that, really. What was making me feel really weird, though, was the idea of not being at Manor Park to cheer on the boys every other Saturday afternoon.

Even if my dad hadn't been at the club for fifteen years and skippered them to promotion to the Premier

League for the very first time, I'd still have been a Shelby Town supporter. I'd still have wanted to be at every home game with my mum and my Uncle George. I'd still have the best memories of winning the Championship Play-Off Final and seeing us reach Wembley again in the Carling Cup final the following season. Plain and simple: Shelby Town was the best thing about growing up, as far as I was concerned. Dad might be able to change clubs, but I couldn't. Not now. And who the hell were Getafe anyway?

That evening, I rushed home from school, hoping Dad would already be there. But there was no sign of him; no car in the garage. Mum was doing something or other with a new set of curtains up in the loft, but when she heard me come in, she shouted down that there was a sandwich on the kitchen table. I grabbed that and sat down in front of the telly, quickly flicked to "Favourites" with the remote and selected Sky Sports News. I watched for a few minutes and then up popped Mr Carstairs talking outside the ground. My heart sank.

This is how it went:

Matt Buckley: *Well, here I am outside Manor Park. Big game here tomorrow night for Shelby Town, of course, at home to Manchester City. A real battle of the haves and the have-nots. But all the talk today has been about skipper Dave Morgan's future. I'm here joined by Ernest Carstairs, the Town Chairman. What's the latest on Dave Morgan, Mr Carstairs?*

Ernest Carstairs: *Well, Mitch—*

Matt Buckley: *It's Matt, Mr Chairman.*

Ernest Carstairs: *Ah, right you are. Sorry, Mike, um, Morgan? Fit for tomorrow night as far as I know.*

Matt Buckley: *But what about the stories linking him with a move to La Liga? Have you spoken to Getafe?*

Ernest Carstairs: *Can't say that I have. We're talking to Dave about a new contract, of course. Wouldn't want to see him leave. But he'll do what's best for him and his family, I'm sure. You know, if Real Madrid or Barcelona came calling, I'd be thinking about it as well. They certainly pay their players bigger wages than Shelby Town can afford.*

Matt Buckley: *Thanks, Mr Chairman. So there we are. The very latest on the Dave Morgan saga. Don't forget, we're at Manor Park for Town versus City tomorrow night. The game's live in HD and 3D, build-up from seven, only on Sky. Back to you, Rob.*

What did he call it? "The Dave Morgan saga"? A tiny bit in the paper on a Tuesday morning and a few hours later it's already a "saga"? I turned off the telly and, just at that moment, Dad walked into the front room. I looked at him, and to me it seemed he was thinking, Does Anthony know? He looked at me and I was thinking, Does he know that I know?

"All right, Dad?" I said.

"*Si, hombre, muy bien!*"

I stared at him. Was he winding me up?

He laughed. "That's 'Yes, mate, very well,' in Spanish. Thought you'd have picked that up from watching the Spanish football on telly. Never know when a bit of *Español* is going to come in handy, do you?"

Suddenly, my mouth was a bit dry and I could feel my eyes pricking. Was I going to start crying? I gulped down some air and said, "What's going on, Dad? Mrs Anderson showed me the newspaper. And I just saw Mr Carstairs on TV."

Dad sat down on the sofa next to me. "What's going on? If I told you, I'd have to kill you, wouldn't I? Never mind all that. How do you think we'll get on at home to City tomorrow?"

"Win, of course. Or we'll have a good go, anyway. It's live on the telly, isn't it? That means everyone'll be talking about it at school on Thursday. All the football experts."

Dad laughed again. Then he ruffled my hair. "Well, you won't have to listen to any of that. You've got a day off school on Thursday. You, me and Mum are going on a little day trip. I've already spoken to the headmaster. But I can't say more than that. All top secret and you never know who might be listening. Come on, let's have a kick-around in the back garden. You can be Lionel Messi and I'll be Iker Casillas."

"No, let's make it *Match of the Day*. I'll be Stuart Dolan and you be Joe Hart."

So we went out into the garden and it was suddenly just like any other afternoon after school. Me and Dad mucking about. Him telling me funny things that had happened at training; me saying I didn't have any homework, even though I did.

Dad wasn't going to let me know what was going on and I knew better than to ask him. I just smashed penalties past him into our mini goal while he did stupid commentary in a funny high-pitched voice. Dad's always known how to make me laugh. And once I was laughing, I wasn't thinking about him leaving Town or us having to leave Shelby any more.

The following evening, me and Mum and Uncle George drove down to Manor Park for the game against City. The game went by in a blur. All around us, I could hear people talking about Dave Morgan and him leaving for Spain on a free transfer at the end of the season. I just shrank down in my seat, hoping nobody would say anything to us. Maybe it was my imagination, but it seemed Mum and Uncle George didn't even realize what was going on. Or they were pretending not to, anyway.

David Silva scored for City in the first half, after Dad slipped over on the edge of the penalty area and let him in on the goal. Some of the crowd got really angry about it, shouting things like: "Keep your mind on the game, Morgan!" And: "You're not off in the sunshine yet!" By half-time, I'd had enough. I didn't know which way to turn. I wanted to have a go back at them. I wanted to ask Mum what was happening with Dad. And, more than anything, I wanted Shelby Town to equalize. It was one of those games when you knew that the next goal would be the important one. If City scored it, with all their big stars, then we might end up getting hammered.

After half-time, Shelby had to defend like lions for fifteen minutes. City came out wanting to finish us off. But we stuck in there. Jim MacDonald made a fantastic save from Vincent Kompany and then we charged up the other end and won a corner. Danny Smith took it and Tom Allenby flicked it on at the near post. Suddenly there was Dad, bundling the ball over the line with his knee from a yard out. Manor Park went bonkers! All of a sudden, the supporters who'd been having a go at him before were singing: "One Dave Morgan! There's only one Dave Morgan!" 1–1 at full-time felt like a victory. Little Shelby Town had got the better of the big boys again.

We got home in time for the highlights on telly. Right at the end of the programme, there was an interview with Dad:

Ross Davies: *Congratulations, Dave. Big goal, that. Your first of the season.*

Dave Morgan: *Well, my job's stopping goals, not scoring them. But after I'd let their lad in for the first* *goal, I thought I'd better do something about it. And even I don't miss from that range. It was a great flick on from Tom.*

Ross Davies: *You were getting a bit of stick from the Manor Park crowd, weren't you?*

Dave Morgan: *Well, that's fair enough. Shows you how far we've come that the supporters aren't happy when we fall behind to a team as good as City, doesn't it?*

Ross Davies: *But what about your future, Dave? Is there anything you can tell us?*

Dave Morgan: *Not really, Ross. The only thing is to remind our fans that they shouldn't believe everything they read in the papers.*

Ross Davies: *Thanks, Dave. Congratulations on your goal. One thing's for sure. Every Shelby Town fan was glad you were here to stick that one away!*

I was already asleep by the time Dad got home. Or, at least, I was already in bed: lying there wondering about the future, wondering about the possibility of a new life in Spain and whether I'd ever get used to not watching Shelby Town. The City game had been brilliant – fight, spirit, all the things that made my club special – and I couldn't really imagine life without nights like that.

I must have nodded off eventually because Mum shook me awake while it was still dark outside. It took me a minute to remember: we were off on a trip today, weren't we? Before I knew it, I was bundled up under a coat on the back seat of the car, half-asleep as we headed for East Midlands airport. I listened to Mum and Dad chatting in the front but couldn't really make out what they were saying. They both sounded pretty excited but I didn't know why. Once we got to the airport, though, I found out what they'd been whispering about. We stood in line at the check-in desk. The electronic display over our heads read "MADRID".

I saw one or two people glancing Dad's way, as if they were trying to work out whether he was who they thought he was. I just sat at the gate with my head buried in the morning paper. The Shelby versus City game was all over the back page. I skimmed through it and then, at the bottom, there was a separate story headlined *MORGAN: THE BIG DECISION*. It talked about Dad's goal, about the fans' reaction to the "news" of him leaving Shelby and about what Town would do if they were to lose their skipper. This was crazy: one minute there was a rumour and the next thing it was as if the deal was already done. I should have been angry. But then I remembered where I was: getting ready to board a plane to Spain. Maybe Dad *had* already made his decision.

When we landed in Madrid, we were met outside the airport by a very friendly old guy with grey hair who spoke perfect English. He introduced himself as Jorge, one of the Vice Presidents of Getafe Club de Fútbol: "Geta" for short. He opened the car door, making a big fuss of seeing Mum in first. I climbed in next to her and Dad sat in the front. We wound our way out through the Madrid traffic and headed off along a ring road that was as big as a motorway. I looked out through the window, trying to make sense of the road signs and the adverts on the billboards, half of which seemed to have something to do with football. I recognized familiar faces like Cristiano Ronaldo and Xabi Alonso, six metres tall and all smiles, selling everything from video games to toothpaste.

In no time at all, we were pulling up outside a football stadium that was right alongside the dual carriageway. A notice outside read "Coliseum Alfonso Perez". Dad spun round in his seat and whispered,

"This is my stop. Jorge is going to take you on a little tour and then we'll meet up again for a slap-up lunch, eh? We've come all this way. Better see the sights and try a bit of the local food." And with that, he was off. There were a couple of guys waiting for him outside the stadium, one in a tracksuit and one in a shiny blue suit. We watched for a moment as he shook hands with them and then disappeared through a doorway which looked like it must be the players' entrance.

Of course, what I really wanted to do was sit down somewhere with Mum and get her to explain what was going on, but instead Jorge drove us into the centre of Madrid. And didn't stop talking for a minute. He pointed to every other building and explained its history. We stopped outside the Bernabéu stadium and he told us all about Real Madrid and how Getafe loved coming to play against the *Galácticos*; how the Getafe fans looked forward to their games there more than any others. The more I listened, the more it sounded as if Getafe were a bit like a Spanish version of Shelby Town: a little club who'd battled their way to the top against all the odds.

A couple of hours later, we were sitting in a restaurant in a big square surrounded by old buildings and apartments. It was plush: all red-leather booths and white tablecloths. Jorge was still talking:

explaining the menu to us and trying to get me to try some squid. I didn't want to be rude but I didn't really feel like eating at all, least of all squid. Just in the nick of time, though, Dad turned up to rescue me. He slid onto the seat alongside me with a big smile on his face:

"How was your tour? What d'you think of Madrid, then?"

Jorge stood up and shook hands with Dad and then with me and Mum. I'd decided I quite liked him, even though he went on a bit. But now he was off.

"Mr Morgan, Mrs Morgan, Anthony, it has been a pleasure welcoming you to Spain. I expect you have a lot of things you want to talk about. I will return in two hours to take you back to the airport. Please enjoy lunch. I have spoken to the restaurant and they will look after you. And, of course, the meal is courtesy of Getafe CF."

Then, all of a sudden, it was just the three of us, looking at each other and wondering who was going to say something first. It had been a strange couple of days: the rumours, the mystery and Dad keeping things secret. Now we were a world away from Shelby, sitting together in a posh restaurant in the capital of Spain. And, like Jorge said, we had some talking to do.

Dad explained everything that had been going on. He talked about Getafe and how they'd phoned up and he'd made all the arrangements because he didn't have an agent. He told us how he'd said to the Getafe President that he didn't think he was cut out for life in Spain. But *El Presidente* had insisted that Dad came out to meet them and have a look around. While Jorge had shown me and Mum round Madrid, he'd met the manager and the players, visited the training ground and talked to the President about the history of the club.

"I've got to say they're absolute gentlemen. No pressure, no talk about money. They already knew everything about me and all about Shelby Town. I don't suppose a chance like this will ever come my way again – or come *our* way again. What d'you think?"

Mum said she was worried about taking me away from school in England, worried about having to learn Spanish, worried about finding a new house, worried about us making new friends a long way from home. But she said that she'd be happy, whatever Dad decided he wanted to do.

Then Dad turned to me, with a serious look on his face. "And what do you think, son?"

I took a deep breath and said it was up to him. But that the one thing I was really scared about was leaving Shelby Town behind. "I know it's just a job to you, Dad. But Town are my team. I can't imagine life without going to games at Manor Park."

Dad twisted round in his seat and looked straight at me. I couldn't tell what he was thinking. Was he angry with me? Did he think I was talking rubbish? He reached across and took Mum's hand, and then turned back to me. "Anthony, you're a funny one. You know Shelby Town's more than a job to me. I've been with the club for my whole career; I've seen them through from non-league into the Prem' and it's been an incredible adventure. But I reckon you'd be a Town fan whether I played for them or not. I actually think the club's even more important to you than it is to me."

I wasn't going to argue with that. But I wasn't going to ruin things for Dad, either. "Whatever you want to do, Dad, that'll be OK. I'd still be able to go back and watch games with Uncle George sometimes, wouldn't I?"

"Of course you would, son. But I'm not sure that'd be the same, would it? Wouldn't be the same for me, anyway."

Dad gave a little chuckle and reached into his coat pocket. He pulled out a white envelope, which had been folded in two, then opened it carefully and laid out some typed sheets on the tablecloth in front of us. The first page was blank except for a couple of lines in the middle, which said:

Agreement between SHELBY TOWN FOOTBALL CLUB LTD and DAVID ANTHONY MORGAN, Footballer

I looked at the paper and then looked at Dad. I could see that Mum had a little smile starting to spread across her face. Dad was still holding her hand. "Well, I can't say I'm not tempted but Shelby Town have always looked after me," he said quietly. "They've offered me a pay rise from the start of next season and the chance to do some coaching with the under-16s at Manor Park, too."

"But what about Getafe, Dad?" I spluttered, hoping Dad was saying what I thought he was saying. "What about coming all the way here? They've even paid for our lunch."

Dad laughed out loud – so loud, the people on the next table turned around. "I told you, these people are gentlemen," he said. "They invited us out here with no strings attached. I've already explained to them that I think my future is still at Manor Park. I thanked them for their hospitality. And I've asked them if they would bring a team over next season to play Town in my testimonial."

With that, Dad turned to the very last sheet of paper laid out on the table in front of us. There were

two dotted lines, the first of which had a squiggle
of a signature in green pen on it and a line of type
underneath:

E Carstairs

....

Ernest Carstairs, OBE, Chairman,
Shelby Town FC

Dad took out his pen and, on the dotted line just below
Mr Carstairs's signature, slowly and carefully signed
his own name:

David Anthony Morgan

....

"Come on then, Anthony," he said. "Jorge'll be
here in a minute. We've got a plane to catch soon.
I've made my decision. Now you've got to make yours.
What's it going to be for afters?"

I leant over and gave Dad a big hug. "Um, I don't
know. Ice cream, maybe. But what I really want…"

Dad grinned. "Yeah? What?"

"Well, if you're staying at Shelby, d'you think you could organize some tickets for me and Mum and Uncle George to come to the away game at Tottenham on Sunday?"

Goalie Acrostic

(Jim MacDonald's poem)

Gargantuan, colossus, often god-like,

Omnipresent guardian of the goal.

A giant amongst mortals, superhuman,

Lord of the area he patrols.

Keeper of the nets – he keeps them empty –

Everything he touches he controls.

Even power blasters or deflections,

Perfect timing, wondrous to behold:

Ever the invincible MacDonald,

Reflexes of lightning, touch of gold.

MURDER AT MANOR PARK!

TOM PALMER

Raphael is a striker at Shelby Town FC's Football Academy. He plays for the under-13s.

This is an excerpt from the diary he writes at the end of every day.

Monday 15 August

A terrible thing has happened at Shelby Town.
Someone is dead!

When I got to the Academy for training tonight,
there were loads of police cars and an ambulance
there. The car park under the main stand had that
police tape around it. And behind the tape was one
of those tents you see on cop shows like *CSI*, the kind
they use to cover up a dead body.

That's what I thought when I first saw the tent
and everything: they're making a film or a TV series
and using Shelby Town as a setting.

So, when I went along to the Academy dressing
rooms and saw Mr Hardaker, the Academy Director,
I said, "They're making a film, aren't they?"

Mr Hardaker was behaving very strangely. He
told me to be quiet and pulled me into his office.

"What's going on?" I asked. I thought I'd done
something wrong. This was what usually happened
before you got told off.

"They're not making a film, Raph," he said.

I just looked at him.

"There's been an accident," he went on.

I carried on looking at him, saying nothing.

"A bad accident," he said. Then he told me.

Someone had fallen from the top of the main stand, where the offices are. Brian Harris, the club's chief scout. The man who goes all over the world to find players for Town.

And he's dead!

Tuesday 16 August

There was no official training tonight. But because it's the start of the season, we're allowed to go down to the Academy and do some extra work: running around the pitches; sprinting; a bit of weight training. That sort of thing.

Dad drove me down after we'd had our tea.

I told him that I wanted to go to Manor Park to do a bit of training on my own. And that was true. Partly true. But I wanted to see what was going on after the accident the day before, too.

Dad dropped me off at the gates, so I had to walk past the main stand again. I know it sounds weird, but I wanted to see the place where Mr Harris had fallen. I could see that the police tent was gone. And the police tape. But when I got near, I suddenly felt like I *didn't* want to see where he'd died. I don't think I was scared. I'm not sure what I was feeling.

So I walked round the edge of the car park, past one of those TV vans: a small minibus with a satellite

dish on top and "Leeside News" on the side, spelt
out in flashy lettering. There was a group of people
standing on the other side of the van: a man with a
camera, and a woman with a big microphone – one
of those big furry ones they stick in a manager's face
after a game. And then another woman. She put her
hand up to tell me to stop, so I stopped.

And I watched.

The reason she'd stopped me was that they were
interviewing someone live. I craned my neck and
saw they were talking to Ralph McGregor. He's
the Commercial Director at Shelby. Whatever a
Commercial Director is.

And, to be honest, I don't like him. He came
down once to take loads of pictures of the under-13s
training. They were for some business deal he was
trying to do for the club. And he was a bit of an idiot,
talking to us like we were kids. I mean, I know we
are kids. We're twelve. But he was talking to us like
we were five or six.

Anyway, I was forced to stand there and listen to
him going on in the way he goes on. He had his hair
all stuck up and was wearing a weird green tie and
green shirt. He looked stupid.

"Mr McGregor, how is the club coping with the
loss of Brian Harris?" asked the interviewer.

"We are all very sad," Ralph McGregor said. "It's a terrible loss. We see Shelby Town as a family. It's like losing a brother." Then he made a strange face. Like he was *trying* to look sad. But he didn't fool me.

"We understand that a sixty-five-year-old man is helping police with their enquiries into this accident," the interviewer said. "Is there any truth in the rumour that Mr Harris's death was more than an accident?"

"I can't comment on that," Ralph McGregor commented. "But I would like to say that we will work very closely with the police. And that the club is very much of a mind that this was an accident. *Clearly* an accident."

I knew who the sixty-five-year-old man they were talking about was. Frank Kendall. He's the only man that old who works at Shelby, apart from the Chairman. Frank is the kit man. But he's more than that, he's always around, helping fix things and taking people places, doing favours. And always nice to the junior players. He had his sixty-fifth birthday at the club a couple of months ago. Hearing Frank was being interviewed by the police worried me.

"Why would they want to interview the sixty-five-year-old man if it was just an accident?" the TV person asked.

"The man in question was the only one in the main stand at the time," Mr McGregor answered. "The police want to talk to him to find out if he saw anything. He's not being interviewed as a suspect. He has not been charged."

"OK," said the interviewer, shifting on her feet. "We also understand that Mr Harris's fiancée works for Shelby Town FC."

"That's true."

"We understand that she is Sandy Lane, the Communications Officer, who normally deals with the media at Shelby Town."

"I have nothing to say about that. My colleague, Miss Lane, is grieving. I refuse to talk about the personal lives of Shelby Town employees like this. I think it best we end the interview here."

So it ended.

But I can't stop thinking about what I heard. People thinking that Mr Harris's fall wasn't an accident. Mr Kendall being interviewed by the police. Was there more to this than I'd first thought? And I was also really confused to hear that Mr Harris was engaged to Sandy Lane. Because I'd thought his girlfriend was Diane Eastham, who runs the Junior Supporter's Club. I saw them together only weeks ago, in a restaurant. And they were holding hands.

Friday 19 August

We had training tonight. The atmosphere was a bit eerie. Everyone wanting to talk about Mr Harris, but no one daring to. Mr Hardaker has said that *no one* should talk about it: not to each other, not to any of the journalists who are outside the main gates.

One of those reporters tried to ask me something when Mum dropped me off for training.

"Hey, son," he said, "any news on Brian Harris's *accident*?"

It was the way he said "accident" that bothered me. Like he thought it *hadn't* been an accident.

Then he shoved a £20 note at me. "Tell us what you know," he said. "There's more where this came from."

I pushed the money away. I wanted to shout at him. To tell him to get lost, that someone had died. But I didn't.

Actual training was good. We were doing shooting: practising how to hit the ball really hard but keep it on target. Mr Hardaker took training for once. He put up some targets and challenged us to knock them over with the ball. I tried as hard as I could and did pretty well.

After training, Mr Hardaker pulled me aside.

I thought I was in trouble. Maybe he'd seen me talking to the journalist.

"You did well in training tonight," he said. "You can hit the ball hard, can't you?"

"Thanks," I said.

"I heard what you did with the journalist earlier, Raph."

I nodded, not sure what to say.

"You were a good lad, turning down money and keeping quiet. The boss saw you do it. He wanted me to pass on his thanks." By the boss, Mr Hardaker meant Mick Diamond, the first-team Manager.

Then Mr Hardaker gave me some match tickets for Shelby's Premier League game against Leeds United, who have just been promoted.

So now I'm really happy.

I showed the tickets to Dad. He said he was proud of me. And now we can go to the match tomorrow.

Saturday 20 August, 4 p.m.

I've just got back from the Leeds match. Except there wasn't a Leeds match. It was called off.

They found another dead body! Another person from Shelby Town.

That's all I could find out. Not who it is. Not what happened. Not anything.

Saturday 20 August, 9 p.m.

There's been loads more on the TV about Shelby
Town. Ralph McGregor was on Sky, BBC and ITV,
talking about what's going on. Because there's more
news out now.

That the second dead person is Diane.
Diane Eastham: the lady who runs the Junior
Supporter's Club.

That it's a murder enquiry. Into her death, and
Brian Harris's.

And that a sixty-five-year-old man has been
arrested and is in custody. Mr Kendall again.
I know it.

I'm finding it hard to believe that he's involved.
But why would they arrest him if he didn't do it?

Dad said it doesn't mean anything. They might
just be asking Mr Kendall about what he knows. That
he probably hasn't been charged with anything.

Dad phoned someone he knows at Shelby Town.
They told him they found Diane Eastham's body in
the cold bath, the one in the first-team's dressing
room that they use when a player's picked up an
injury. They said she'd been held down under the
water: drowned. And that her body was blue when
they discovered it.

Sunday 21 August

The Sunday paper Dad gets says that another man has been arrested at Shelby Town FC. And that he's going to be charged with a double murder. A man in his twenties. So it's *not* Mr Kendall.

They said their newspaper had been sent an anonymous letter telling them that *this* man was the murderer. And that they had evidence to prove it.

I wondered if it was one of the first-team players. Most of them are in their twenties.

I'm really confused.

Dad said not to believe what I read in the newspapers. He said half of it's made up and the other half's full of mistakes. He said I should keep an open mind.

But who is it? Who's the murderer? That's what I want to know.

Monday 22 August

Training was cancelled again tonight. There was a big sign up on the gates at Manor Park.

I feel weird. Playing for the Academy and following the Town first team is my life. And now everything has stopped.

The evening paper headline was *WHO'S NEXT AT SHELBY TOWN?* Like they thought someone else was going to be killed.

Just as I was leaving the ground – once I'd found out training was cancelled – I saw Mr Hardaker. He said it was a shame I hadn't been able to see Shelby play Leeds, but that I'd get another chance.

I said I was sorry about Mr Harris and Miss Eastham, and told him I'd seen them together in a restaurant I'd been to with Mum and Dad. That's why I'd thought Mr Harris was going out with Miss Eastham and not Miss Lane.

Mr Hardaker looked surprised. "You saw Mr Harris with Miss Eastham?" he asked.

I nodded.

"Don't you mean Mr Harris and Miss Lane?"

"No," I said. "It was definitely Miss Eastham."

Mr Hardaker frowned. "Are you sure?"

"Yes," I said. "I know her because I'm a member of the Junior Supporter's Club."

"I think I need to talk to Miss Lane," Mr Hardaker said, looking at his watch. "Tomorrow. It'll have to be tomorrow now."

"D'you think she might be next?" I asked. And immediately wished I hadn't, because it made Mr Hardaker look sad.

Then he gave me a smile. The kind of smile adults give children when they think we don't understand things.

And it was odd, because he said just what Dad had said: "Don't always believe what you read in the newspapers, Raph."

Tuesday 23 August

The summer holidays are nearly over. I woke up this morning wondering what to do. Mum and Dad had both gone to work. I had the house to myself.

I got a pint of milk out of the fridge and put the TV on.

Chat shows.

Cookery shows.

News.

I'd had enough of news, so I switched it off.

There was one of my mum's books on the table next to the sofa. *Love Triangle*, it was called.

I picked it up and read the blurb. *Cassie loves Jed. But she's promised to Pete. What should she do? Break Pete's heart and be happy herself? Or live a lie?*

This is rubbish, I thought. Some crappy love story. I put the TV news back on. Anything was better than a love story.

But the news was still all about Shelby Town: live images taken through the closed front gates. Gates that are three metres high, made of iron.

The camera scanned the offices in the stadium while the news reporter spoke. I looked to see if I could spot anyone through the windows, but the offices seemed to be empty. Then the camera panned down the hill to the right, towards the Academy playing fields.

And that was where I *did* see someone I knew.

Mr Hardaker. Walking across one of the pitches. But not towards the Academy: he was walking towards the other offices. The ones that stand apart from the stadium, where the media centre is based. Where Sandy Lane's office is.

And my heart started beating faster.

I sat up.

Suddenly I had that feeling I get before a game for the Academy. The excitement. The adrenalin. But sitting here it wasn't a good feeling. On the pitch, you can run it off. Use it. But sitting on the sofa at my house? Why was I feeling like this now?

I looked at the TV. I could still see Mr Hardaker walking down to the media centre.

And then I knew.

WHO'S NEXT AT SHELBY TOWN?

Love Triangle.

Brian Harris...

Diane Eastham...

Sandy Lane...

And Mr Hardaker. He was going to talk to Sandy Lane. To help her.

But what if ... what if she was ... the one who killed Mr Harris and Miss Eastham?

I ran to the stadium. At a medium pace, so I'd have some energy left when I got there. And I still had the adrenalin.

But was I being crazy? Thinking that Miss Lane could be a danger to Mr Hardaker? And that, because we'd talked about it yesterday, I had sent him there.

I'd told him I thought Brian Harris was going out with Miss Eastham, not Miss Lane, and he was going to warn her. But warn her about what? He must have thought she was in danger.

I wasn't sure. How could I be? But I had a real gut feeling.

As I got near to the stadium, my mind was telling me to stop. To turn round and go home. The police had someone in custody, didn't they? The man in his twenties.

But I couldn't stop. Because my heart was saying, *Carry on.*

When I reached the stadium gates, there was a large van coming out. The two men on the gate were helping it to reverse. So I just darted in, running around the side of it as it rolled backwards. I was through the car park in seconds, sprinting now.

Once I was on the pitches, I headed straight for the media centre. That was where I'd watched Mr Hardaker go less than ten minutes ago, on TV.

My chest was heaving. My legs felt stiff. Not enough oxygen in my blood. I needed a rest.

But I kept on.

I *had* to keep on.

And then I saw them.

Just in front of the side door.

Mr Hardaker was facing someone who had her back to me.

And they were just talking: nothing dramatic. It was Miss Lane and Mr Hardaker.

Everything was going to be all right. I'd been stupid. *What was I doing here?*

I stopped and put my hands on my knees, gasping and trying to draw breath, staring at a discarded ball that was sitting on the grass just ahead of me.

And then I saw Miss Lane turn slightly,

something in her hands. Like a broom handle.
Except it wasn't a broom handle.

It was a gun.

An air rifle. Something like that. And she was
pointing it at Mr Hardaker.

That was when Mr Hardaker looked away from
the gun, seeing me for the first time.

"Go!" he shouted. Shouted to *me*! "Get out of here!"

But that was all he could shout, because
Miss Lane hit him over the head with the gun and
he went down on the floor. He fell hard, as if he'd
been tackled by John Terry.

Then Sandy Lane began to turn towards *me*, the
gun swinging round in her hands. Soon it would be
pointing at me.

I found myself running, but not away from her.
Towards her. And towards the ball on the grass.

Before the gun was pointing at me, I was onto
the ball. And I hit it. Hard and accurate, just like
Mr Hardaker had taught me.

The ball flew at her. She tried to move out of its
path, but there was no time. The ball hit her in the
face, full on. The gun just dropped out of her hands,
followed by a huge bang, bullets flying everywhere.

Then Mr Hardaker was on top of her, pulling
her hands behind her back.

The two security guys from the main gate were racing across the pitches now.

And when I looked at Mr Hardaker, after a long silence that seemed to echo with gunshots, he smiled. Then he said, "Good shot, Raph. Good shot."

Wednesday 24 August

I'm grounded. Watching TV with my dad.

There are no newspaper journalists and TV cameras outside Shelby Town FC now. They're all outside our house instead.

They're here for me. I'm supposed to be a hero. But I wish they'd go away.

My dad read the paper to me this morning. Sandy Lane has been charged with the murders of Brian Harris and Diane Eastham. According to the gossip on a website I read, she killed Mr Harris by accident. But she thought Miss Eastham knew she'd done it because she'd found out they were having an affair behind her back, so she killed her, too. This time, on purpose.

Then she lost it. Really lost it. And when Mr Hardaker came to help her, she decided she was going to kill him, too.

But Dad says I shouldn't believe what I read on the Internet.

Saturday 27 August

It's Shelby Town FC vs. Arsenal today. I've been given tickets for the match, as a thank you for saving Mr Hardaker's life and working out who the murderer was. In fact, I've got two tickets to every Shelby Town FC game for ever. Home or away.

They're presenting me with a golden season ticket in front of the crowd. I didn't want to go out in front of 30,000 people, but Mr Hardaker said that I might have to get used to it if I carried on doing well at the Academy.

So I said I hoped that by the time I was eighteen I wouldn't need one of the tickets. Because I hoped that I'd be going out on the pitch again one day.

As a Shelby Town player.

No One Gets Past Me

(Dave Morgan's poem)

I'm a blaster, not a tapper,
A ninety-minute scrapper,
A chopper and a hacker. I don't shave!
I've got the brawn and muscle
For the tackle and the tussle,
I will hassle and I'll hustle: I'm Big Dave.

Harum-scarum, do-or-dare 'em,
I will take the knocks and bear 'em.
Show me strikers and I'll scare 'em to the grave.
I'm a winner, not a loser,
A rough 'em, tough 'em bruiser,
A goal scorer's confuser: I'm Big Dave.

Summer sun or winter mire,
Lion-hearted do or die er,
In my belly burns a fire: so behave!
I'm a last-ditch tackle fighter,
A knee and ankle biter.
Nobody marks you tighter: I'm Big Dave.

Big and bulky, bold and brave,

Nobody gets past Big Dave.

Like a force-ten tidal wave,

Nobody gets past Big Dave.

I will stop and I will save

The day because I am Big Dave!

ONE KATY JACKSON

FAYE WHITE

I suppose it should make me feel a bit jealous. I mean, is there a boy anywhere who loves football who hasn't dreamt about playing for England? Even if it's never going to happen? Well, it was never going to happen to me. But Katy? It's there in black and white, the headline at the top of the story in the local paper:

LEESIDE GIRL GETS ENGLAND CALL-UP!

Kate Jackson, just 16 years old and from the Northwick Estate in Shelby, has been called into the England Women's squad for the upcoming international friendly against France at Leicester City's King Power Stadium in two weeks' time.

That's Kate Jackson. Sister of Alan Jackson. Sister of me. How could I not be jealous of her? She'll be running out in the white shirt, the Three Lions on her chest, in front of thousands of people and the TV cameras. I'll be there. So will Mum and Dad. So will half of Shelby, I'll bet. They'll be proud of her and I will be too.

Now this is supposed to be my *little* sister I'm talking about. Except she's not so little, actually. She never has been. Even when I was ten or eleven, Katy – eighteen months younger – was already as tall as I was. And she's not stopped growing since. Only sixteen and skinny as a rake but she's nearly six feet tall.

So, when we were growing up, nobody ever thought of her as my "little" sister. She was as tall as us boys and she was better than most of us at football. Not that we ever said that to her. But you could tell we all knew, when it came to picking sides in the school playground or over in the park. Whoever was captain would always make sure they picked Katy first.

Katy just always wanted to play. I can remember her volunteering to go in goal for me in the back garden when she was only four or five. And she was keen: when I put the ball through one of the kitchen windows, she told Mum she'd done it. I'd promised her that I'd go in goal for a bit if she did, and Katy would do anything to be the one taking shots for a change.

So when Dad started a team on the estate for me and my mates, of course Katy wanted to be involved. All the boys were a couple of years older than her, but she'd come along to our games with her best friend, Jackie, who loved football too. The pair of them would run up and down the touchline, cheering us on. They'd sprint off across the pitches to get the ball when it went out of play. It was a bit embarrassing: your sister shouting out what you should be doing in the middle of games.

Sometimes Dad would give Katy and Jackie one of our spare balls, and they'd find a few kids around the park to start a game of their own with: two-a-side, five-a-side against whoever they could find, stray dogs included. And every Tuesday they came along to our training sessions. They'd join in, do everything we did, and then give us the runaround when Dad finished up with a small-sided match. Jackie was smaller and quicker but Katy could do the lot. When she tackled you, you stayed tackled. Midfield or up front, she could play anywhere: chasing back, clearing the ball off the line and then running up the other end to score.

Us boys were always pretending we were superstars off the telly, playing for Shelby Town or Man United or Chelsea. Katy was different: she never pretended to be anybody and she was always serious about winning.

It never made sense to me that she couldn't play in our team once we all turned eleven. She was as good as us. Why did the rules say she couldn't play with the boys?

I know Dad felt bad about that too. I still remember him talking to her after training one night, explaining that we were too old now and that she wouldn't be able to play with us any more. Katy was upset about it but I think Dad was even more upset. It ended up with Katy putting her arm around *his* shoulder and telling him he shouldn't worry, that everything would be OK.

Funnily enough, it was Mum who came to the rescue. We were having our tea a couple of nights later and she pulled out this leaflet from the leisure centre that was advertising girls' football sessions. I don't think Katy had ever really thought about there being "girls'" football. She just played; she wasn't too sure about the "girls'" bit. But as soon as Jackie said she was up for it, Katy agreed.

Well, I don't want to sound too dramatic. But it was pretty dramatic. You could say that night at the leisure centre changed Katy's life. The coach who was taking the session, John Pullman, was involved with the ladies' team at Shelby Town, which had only just started up. They'd set up a reserve team as well – a "development squad", John called it. He only needed one look. Straight after that first session at the leisure centre, he was asking Katy and Jackie if they wanted to come along for trials.

Of course Shelby Town wanted to take Katy and Jackie on. Even though they were younger than everyone else at the club. The reserves were really a youth team. All the other girls were still at school too, and came from all over Leeside. Almost overnight, everything seemed to change for Katy. Dad's not a bad coach, but John had done all his badges and everything: Katy was learning something new every training session. And she was playing for a proper team, in proper games, even if they were friendlies.

Us boys kept playing too. Dad put us into the local youth league and everything, but to be honest we were just messing about. Football was something we did for fun at the weekend. But for Katy it all started getting serious as soon as she joined Shelby Town. She was always the first at training. John made her captain of the team. I think, even back then, Katy was seeing that now she'd discovered girls' football, she could really do something in the game.

The rest of us never really imagined what that "something" might be. The months rolled by. I suppose we just took it for granted: playing for Shelby Town reserves was just Katy's thing and we let her get on with it. Mum or Dad would take her along to training and to games at the weekend, but we didn't have any proper idea of what might happen. I mean, nobody took girls' football that seriously, did they?

But then, one Sunday afternoon, they had an open day at Shelby Town and a game between the women's first team and the women's reserves was part of the show. We all went down to watch. There were probably a few hundred other people there too. Normally they might not have watched women's football, but the match was on the pitch at Manor Park so they hung around. The manager of Shelby Town ladies' team was there – Denise Rogers. So was the Town manager, Mick Diamond.

Even though Katy and Jackie and their teammates were much younger and less experienced, they played pretty well. Katy scored an amazing goal from the edge of the box, a curler into the top corner, and I remember thinking, Blimey! Is that my sister? Just as the game finished, this old bloke – quite posh – came up to Mum and Dad. He introduced himself: "Ernest Carstairs, Chairman of Shelby Town." They were chatting about the game and then Dad pointed Katy out. Do you know what Mr Carstairs said? "That girl will play for England one day." And do you know what me and Mum and Dad did? We just laughed.

We weren't laughing a couple of nights later, though, when Denise Rogers turned up at our house.

Mum and Dad had been expecting her but I don't think Katy knew she was coming. When the doorbell rang, she and Jackie were upstairs on the PS3 playing *FIFA*. A couple of minutes later, everybody was sitting around the kitchen table. Except me: I had to make the tea and get the biscuits out. And then stand in the corner, listening to every word.

Denise Rogers came straight out with it. Even though Katy and Jackie were still youngsters, she wanted to get them involved with the ladies' first team. It would mean extra training and playing against women instead of other girls. But she thought they were ready for it. I looked at Katy and I knew exactly what she was thinking: she was biting her lip to stop herself shouting out "YES!" straight away. Mrs Rogers said not to rush, that Katy and Jackie should have a chat about what they wanted to do.

The girls disappeared up to Katy's room as soon as Mrs Rogers had gone, and Mum and Dad left them to it. About an hour later, we heard the front door shut and Katy came into the sitting room. We all turned round, expecting to see her with a big grin on her face, but instead she was as white as a sheet. She sat down and stared at the telly. Mum and Dad looked at each other, not knowing what to say, so it was up to me to ask what was wrong.

Well, it turned out that Katy was desperate to join the Shelby first team but that Jackie wasn't. This was her best mate, the mate she'd always played football with. But Jackie wanted to stay with the reserves, with girls more her own age. She was having fun as things were and didn't want to spoil it by moving up to the first team. I thought maybe that would make Katy have second thoughts. But she didn't have any. She'd just told Jackie that she was going to move on and join the first team anyway, even if it meant leaving her best friend behind.

Well, from then on, Katy was still Katy – she was still my "little" sister – but everything else seemed completely different. Instead of playing football with girls and against girls, Katy's world was all about adults all of a sudden. She was only fifteen but the women she was playing with had husbands and children and jobs. They had grown-up lives. They were tough, experienced players and, at first, we weren't sure whether Katy would cope.

Of course she was good enough. Mrs Rogers knew that; otherwise she wouldn't have asked Katy to make the step up to the first team. And Katy could handle herself, too. Having played so much football against boys had made sure of that. But she'd never had pressure on her before: a game every week, wearing the

Shelby Town shirt, reports in the local paper and the Town programme, a battle against relegation to stay in the league. She started having anxiety attacks before games and getting all dizzy during them, feeling as if she was going to pass out.

Dad talked to her. Mum talked to her. Mrs Rogers talked to her. I didn't talk to her: I just told her she should go to the doctor's. And, for once, Katy listened to me instead of anyone else. Everybody thought it was the pressure of playing grown-up football. But the doc did some tests and it turned out that Katy wasn't struggling with nerves; she was struggling with growing up. Sixteen and over six feet tall was a bit too much, too quick, for her body to deal with. The doctor said not to worry about it: Katy had to try to get some more sleep. And to eat extra chips.

After that, she still felt wobbly before games; even during them. But now she knew what was going on, she was able to control it a bit, and she wasn't scared of it any more. Actually, Katy wasn't scared of anything. Which is probably why Mrs Rogers started playing her in defence. Playing with us and with the Shelby reserves, Katy had always been the star centre forward or the one running games from midfield. But now she was playing centre half: winning headers and smashing into strikers for ninety minutes at a time.

She loved it. Loved the whole thing. Even though she didn't have that much in common with the older women in the team, they looked after her a bit. Not out on the pitch, where Katy could look after herself, thanks very much, but in the dressing room before and after games. They made a fuss of her when she made mistakes and took the mickey out of her whenever she thought she was playing well. They weren't like Jackie had been: they weren't her mates. But she trusted them. And, when it came to defending, they trusted her.

I don't really know if Katy had a plan for football or whether it was football that had a plan for her. In what seemed like just a couple of years, she'd gone from thinking that she might have lost her chance to play football to being involved in a proper team at Shelby Town. Now Katy's one of the first names on the team sheet, and this season that's meant being part of a Shelby Town side pushing for promotion to the Women's Premier League.

And, as if all that wasn't enough, when the draw was made for the Women's FA Cup, Shelby Town's name came out of the hat just before Arsenal's: home to the Cup holders, the Premier League champions. Katy was beside herself. I couldn't get much sense out of her, except her telling me that it meant she'd be marking

Kelly Smith. I'm not exactly an expert on women's football, so Katy had to take a deep breath and explain to me that playing against Kelly Smith was like playing against Wayne Rooney or Robin van Persie.

If ever Katy was going to feel wobbly before a game, I thought it would be before the game against Arsenal. But she was fine. Only sixteen, but playing against the best team in the country and marking the England centre forward wasn't going to be a problem at all. And it wasn't, either. Town got beaten 3–1 but Kelly Smith didn't score and Katy did, with a header from a corner. You've never seen celebrations like it, on or off the pitch. Me and Mum and Dad were dancing a little jig together when the Town chairman, Mr Carstairs, appeared out of nowhere with a big grin on his face, waggling a finger in the air as if to say, I told you so!

Afterwards, Katy was the only person who wasn't celebrating. She couldn't understand people being happy when Town had lost, however well their centre half had played. But I could tell, deep down, she knew she'd done OK. When her big test had come, she'd passed with flying colours. People were gossiping straight after the game, saying that Arsenal would be coming in to try and sign Katy for next season. Well, that didn't happen. Not straight away, anyway. But what did happen was even better.

A letter dropped onto the doormat at the end of the week. It was half-term so we were all at home. When the letterbox clattered, Katy came rushing downstairs, picked up the envelope addressed to her and sprinted back up to her room. What was going on? I stood at the bottom of the stairs, listening: silence for about a minute and then a thump, followed by a little scream. I went up and burst into Katy's room. There was my sister, lying on the floor – the "thump" had been her falling off her bed – and waving the letter in the air.

I asked what the matter was and Katy just made a squeaking noise. So I grabbed the letter and had a look for myself. The Football Association logo was at the top of it and the signature at the bottom was *Hope Powell*, who, Katy explained to me, was the manager of the England women's national team. Next thing I knew, I was lying on the floor next to my sister and squeaking as well. Who'd have believed it? Kate Jackson, international footballer!

So we're all off up the M1 to Leicester tomorrow night. Katy's been on the phone saying how fantastic the training has been. And telling us not to get our hopes up: the manager's told her she'll be on the bench and will just get a little run-out if the game's going well. But who cares? Even if it's just a minute at the end, we'll all be there to see it: my sister playing for England.

Jealous? Me? Well, maybe a bit. But, most of all, I'm just proud. *Come on, Katy Jackson! Come on, England!* That's my little sister out there, you know.

HALF-TIME TEAM TALK

(Mick Diamond's poem)

This half-time team talk has been censored
Basically it all boils down to
Get out there, get at 'em and pull yer fingers out

Obviously, there are a lot more words than that
Not many you'd say in front of Grandma
And some that are difficult to spell

All the words are angry
All the words are loud
And most of the words are repeated

Still, it must have worked
We scored two goals and stepped it up
Result

DISAPPEARED

HILARY FREEMAN

Sunday

"All right?"

That was the very last thing I said to Holly.

"All right?"

I'm not sure what, if anything, I meant by it; I'm not even sure how to spell it. It's one of those things that you say when you're passing someone on the stairs and you can't help making eye contact. It's the sort of phrase that just pops out of your mouth, a bit like a belch or a burp, but with letters attached.

Whatever I meant, Holly didn't reply. And now nobody knows where she is, or who she's with, or when she's coming back. *If* she's coming back at all. Which is why I'm sitting here on my bed, thinking about the last "conversation" we had before she vanished into thin air, or disappeared off the face of the earth, or went off the radar – wherever it is that people go when they're not where they're supposed to be.

I didn't know anything was up until last night, when I got home from Dad's. We'd spent the afternoon at football, like we do most Saturdays. Buying me a Shelby Town season ticket for my birthday, along with one for himself, was Dad's idea of father–son bonding. He didn't bother to ask me whether I wanted it, or if I'd prefer something else instead. He thought it was just the best present any father could give his son.

If he'd been around for the past five years, he'd know I don't support Shelby Town any more. I went off them around the same time Dad went off Mum (and off with his other woman). I switched my allegiance to Man United instead. I was going to set him straight but, when I saw the proud look on his face as I tore open the envelope, I didn't have the heart to disappoint him. I just said, "Cheers, Dad," and let him swat me across the shoulders.

And so, almost every other Saturday, at one o'clock, he parks up outside Mum's front door, beeps his horn twice to let me know he's arrived, takes me to the match, feeds me as much junk food as I can stuff in, and then drops me home again.

Yesterday's was a particularly boring nil–nil match, and all those hot dogs and onion rings gave me serious wind, so when Dad took me home I was hoping for a quiet night in with my Wii. I'd hardly had time to put my key in the front door lock before Mum was in my face, gripping on to me by the shoulders of my jacket and not letting go. She was shrieking at me.

"Have you seen your sister? Do you know where she is? Has she called you?"

"No!" I shouted back, trying to shake her off me.

She was so close that droplets of her saliva were showering my face.

"I've been at football with Dad. You know I have."

But she just kept on asking, "Are you sure she didn't say anything? Can't you think of something? She must have mentioned something!"

Mum isn't the hysterical type. She's usually calm and tough and quite dry with it. Seeing her all panicky, her voice high-pitched and desperate, made me want to go straight back out the front door again.

"No, Mum," I said, too embarrassed to look her in the eye. "I dunno where she is. What's going on? The last time I saw her was yesterday morning before school. She didn't tell me anything."

I was going to add "She never tells me anything", but I thought better of it.

Mum was clasping my jacket so tightly that the zip at my collar was starting to strangle me. "Let go now, Mum," I pleaded. But it didn't seem as if she could hear me. It was like she was possessed. "Get off me, Mum!" I shouted, as loudly and clearly as I could. I made a sudden jerking motion and, finally, she had to release me.

The jolt seemed to bring her to her senses. "Holly's missing," she said in a quiet voice, her eyes unfocused. "Nobody's seen her since she left school yesterday. I can't get her on her phone and she isn't with any of her friends."

• • •

Last night felt like the longest night in history. I kept out of Mum's way while she phoned everybody in her address book. The police and all the local hospitals, too. After each call she tried Holly's mobile again, although by her fifth attempt she'd given up leaving desperate messages. At some point, the police came round to take a missing person's report. Dad came by and so did some of our neighbours. By ten o'clock I realized there wasn't going to be any dinner cooked, so I sorted myself out with some toast, which I ate alone in my room. There are still crumbs everywhere, even under my duvet.

I honestly did think that Mum was overreacting. Holly's always coming back later than she's supposed to, or calling to say she's staying at a friend's house. I expected her to walk in the front door at any moment so that she and Mum could have an almighty row. Every time I heard a noise, or a car drew up outside, or the phone rang, I thought, There's Holly, at last. Everything can go back to normal.

But now it's Sunday afternoon and she's still not back, and I'm starting to wonder if something really has happened to her. I keep going over that moment on the stairs, in case there's something I missed, a code I haven't been able to break or a look I didn't register. As last words go, "All right?" is pretty lame, isn't it? It's not a great parting shot – hardly up there with "Live long and prosper!" or "May the force be with you!". If I'd just said something as simple as "Have a good day" or "Take care of yourself", at least I'd know that I'd wished her well. Wished her something. Instead, I'd wished her nothing at all.

Monday

So my twin sister's gone missing, and I can't even get out of school for a day. Dad said I had to go.

"Keep you out of trouble," he said. "Your mum's in no state to look after you."

Everyone's heard what's happened. When a fifteen-year-old girl goes missing, the news spreads fast. People are treating me like I'm an alien that's been beamed down into the classroom from the planet Zog. They're staring at me – and whispering about me – whenever they think I'm not looking. Any minute now, I'm expecting someone to get out a probe and hold me down for an internal examination.

I know what people are saying: "Holly's run off with some guy", "She's pregnant", "She's lying in a ditch somewhere". Some of the boys in my year are making nasty jokes, saying disgusting things, stuff

I don't want to think about, let alone repeat. These are things that happen on the news, to other people. Not in real life. Not to my family.

When we were little, Holly and I used to stay up late at night to tell each other scary stories about witches and demons and bogeymen. We'd take it in turns to lock each other in our bedroom in the dark, while the one standing outside made ghostly scrapes and bangs and horrible groaning noises. The first person to be so spooked that they couldn't handle it any more was the loser. I was always better at this game than Holly because the monsters I dreamt up were bigger and scarier. They had teeth that could bite your head clean off, or claws that could slice you in two. They had revolving heads with two faces – one normal, one so horrible it would blind you – or they had necklaces made of children's finger bones. What if she's that scared now, and this time for good reason? What if she's locked inside a dark room and there's nobody to let her out? What if the bogeyman with the bony necklace has got her?

"Oi!" Robbie Bowen has lumbered over, the only person brave – or stupid – enough to talk to me. "So, I was wondering, are you and Holly identical twins?" he asks. "'Cos it might help. You know, looking for her, I mean."

I give him the evils. Is he serious? It's hard to tell with Robbie. Identical? Come on, I'm a bloke for God's sake – how can we be identical? Do I need to get my equipment out to prove it?

"Yeah," I say. "We're identical. You can't tell us apart."

"Oh, right," says Robbie. "So can you, like, read each other's minds? Are you psychopathic?"

Idiot. People always ask me this, along with the identical twin question. Mum likes to think it's true. According to family legend, when we were five, at the exact moment Holly fell off the top of the slide at the playground, I started screaming about a pain in my shin. I've heard it told so often that I don't know if I can actually remember it happening or if I've just imagined myself into the story.

"Yeah, Robbie," I say, closing my eyes. "We're telepathic. I know exactly where she is and who she's with. I'm reading her thoughts right now. I decided I wouldn't tell the police just so they'd have something to do."

He snarls at me. "Only trying to help," he says.

I shrug. All I know is that when Holly went missing on Friday evening, I didn't feel a thing. That night, I got my best-ever score on *Medieval War Games III*, ate almost an entire roast chicken and then slept a full, satisfying ten hours. I didn't think about Holly once. Maybe that means she's OK and nothing bad has happened to her. Or maybe we're just not telepathic.

Tuesday

My phone is ringing.

"Yeah?" I say.

There's a pause and, for a split second, I think it might be Holly and I realize I'm holding my breath. Then I hear a voice that I don't recognize, a soft girl's voice.

"Is that Sam?" asks the voice.

I breathe out silently. "Yeah," I say, trying not to sound disappointed, or irritated. Obviously, it's Sam. Why do people ask that when they've just dialled your number?

"Oh, right. It's Belle here."

She pauses.

"You know, Holly's friend."

"All right?" I say, because I'm not sure how to respond, and because old habits die hard. The truth is I'm shocked. Belle has never called me before. I'm not even sure how she got my number.

"Um..." There's a tiny crack in Belle's voice. "Um, it's, er, about Holly. Can I come round?"

"Yeah," I say. "I guess."

"The thing is, I think your mum's a bit upset with me 'cos Holly said she was supposed to be staying at mine, when she wasn't, on Friday."

"Mum's asleep," I tell her. "Doctor's given her some pills."

"Oh, right." She sounds relieved. "So, can I come right now?"

"If you like."

I hang up. She doesn't take long. I wait in my room for a few minutes, and by the time I get downstairs she's already standing there outside the front door. The frosted glass blurs her silhouette, making her look like a smudged drawing. I open the door and watch as she comes into focus in front of me.

It's two hours later and we're standing at the bottom of a block of flats in the centre of town, waiting for the lift. It stinks of wee and there's graffiti all over the walls. I can't imagine Holly ever coming here, but Belle says different. Belle's told me a lot of stuff that's taken me by surprise. I feel sad, like I don't really know my sister at all.

The lift deposits us on the fifth floor. Then it's a short walk down a grey corridor to a grey front door that looks like every other front door we've passed. Belle raps on the frame with the side of her chunky ring. "Buzzer doesn't work," she explains. "Never has."

Eventually, the door opens. "Oh, it's you," says a guy, tall and pale and unshaven. He's at least nineteen or twenty. "I thought I told you and your mates not to come round."

"It's about Holly," says Belle, peering round the door as if she's trying to see if Holly's inside.

The guy glances around him suspiciously. "Right, yeah, I'd heard. Well, you'd better come in," he says, pulling back the door. Belle walks inside and I follow her. The guy blocks my path with his arm.

"Who are you?"

"I'm Sam. Holly's brother."

"Right," he says. "I'm Rick. OK, then, come in."

We all walk into his living room, where there's a sofa and an armchair, but he doesn't offer us a seat.

"Look," he says to me, "I'm sorry your sister's gone missing, but what you doing here?"

"*What am I doing here?* I'm here because Belle asked me to come with her, because she was scared to come on her own."

"We thought Holly might be here," says Belle. "She told me she was coming to see you on Friday."

"Jesus," says Rick. "Have you told anyone else this?"

"No, course not," says Belle. She's trembling a little.

"Look," says Rick again, "she came round here Friday, yeah, but I told her I didn't want to see her. I told her to go home. I didn't even let her in the flat."

"I don't believe you."

"Believe what you want, love. I didn't let her in. I didn't know she was gonna disappear after, did I?"

Belle looks confused and slightly panicked. "But Holly told me you were her boyfriend now. She says you've been hanging out."

Rick snorts. "In her dreams," he says.

I clench my fist inside my pocket. I want to hit him.

"Nothing happened. Soon as I found out how old she really was, I told her where to go. That was weeks ago. Not my fault if she didn't want to hear it. She's been stalking me ever since."

He takes his phone out of his pocket. "You want proof, just look at this."

He shows us his text folder. There are about eighty messages, all from Holly, all saying "Please call me" and other stuff that makes me cringe. Some of the texts aren't even opened.

Now Belle looks shocked, as if she's realized she didn't really know Holly either.

"So where did she go on Friday then? Where's she been going when she said she was seeing you?"

"I dunno," he says, holding up his hands. "If I knew, I'd tell you, wouldn't I?"

"You're lying," says Belle. "We could go to the police if we wanted." She sounds uncertain.

"Yeah?" says Rick, like he wants to laugh. "And tell them what? I've got plenty of mates who'll swear I'm telling the truth."

Now I want to get out of there. I'm feeling claustrophobic and uncomfortable. I don't like Rick and I don't trust him, and I don't understand why my sister would want anything to do with him.

"We should go," I say to Belle.

"Yeah, you should," says Rick, nodding towards the door. "Hope you find your sister, mate."

In the corridor outside the flat, Belle is quiet and thoughtful. I'm suddenly aware that I hardly know her and that I don't know what to say to her. I press the button for the lift. It's been waiting for us; the doors open immediately.

"Let's get out of here," she says. She looks like she might cry but doesn't want to do it in front of me.

I press "G" for Ground and step backwards.

There's a grinding noise and the lift shakes and jolts into motion. And then, as it begins to pick up speed, there's another jolt, and the lights flash off, and we're in blackness. Just as I'm about to say "God, we're stuck", the lift starts moving again and I'm aware of a horrible plummeting sensation in the pit of my stomach as we rush towards the ground, falling faster and faster down the shaft, as if the lift has broken free of its cables and is never going to stop. I flail against the wall, grasping helplessly for something to hold on to, calling Belle's name. But there's nothing to grip, and my voice isn't coming out, and I can't see Belle and I know that it's hopeless...

And then everything's still. The doors are open and we're at the ground floor, with graffiti and sunlight creeping across the walkways.

"God," I say, shivering. "That was horrible. Are you OK, Belle? Are you hurt?"

"What you talking about, Sam? I'm fine. Nothing's happened, has it? You look terrible. Like you've seen a ... like you've had a shock."

"But the lift ... we were falling."

Belle looks at me sideways, like I'm a crazy person. "No, we weren't," she says. "You must've imagined it. It just got stuck for a second. It's always doing that."

I lean against the wall, steadying myself, catching my breath. I feel freezing cold, inside and out, and my head is banging. I don't know what just happened. But there's one thing I do know, one thing that suddenly seems absolutely, horribly clear. I can't explain it, but I'm now one hundred per cent certain that my sister is dead.

Thursday

I haven't told anyone what I know, or what I felt. What I feel. They wouldn't want to hear it and I'm not sure anyone would take much notice of me. It's not like I've got real evidence; and everyone's too busy running around being practical to listen.

Someone said there's going to be a reconstruction on a TV crime show, with an actress pretending to be Holly. And, at the match next Saturday, Shelby Town are holding a benefit for her: raising money to help with the search. It's kind of ironic; Holly hates football. But she's always wanted to be on TV. Even if she'd be really annoyed that someone else is playing her. They'd better choose someone pretty, or Holly will ... Holly would kill them. She'd come back and haunt them, I'm telling you.

Me? I'm just waiting. Going to school and going straight home after. Watching out of my window.

Listening. Keeping out of Mum's way. Trying not to talk to anyone, in case I upset them. Or in case they think I'm nuts, like Belle does. I feel weird, empty inside; numb. I feel doomed. I know nothing's ever going to be the same again. I know that in a few minutes – in a few hours or a few days – I'm going to be proved right, even though I don't want to be. Every time I hear a car in the street, I think it's them – the police – coming back to give Mum the terrible news. Every time I switch on the TV I expect to hear that they've found a body at the bottom of a lift shaft. A girl's body, in a tower block, not far from here...

You know when people say the silence is deafening? I get that now. There's only a thin wall between Holly's bedroom and mine, a partition made of plywood which some builder mate of Dad's put in. When I move around, I swear I can hear the echo of my own footsteps, as if there's a giant, empty cavern next door. I feel I should whisper and tiptoe as if I'm in church.

There's a car driving up the street. I don't need to look out of the window to know that it's a police car; it has that police car sound, even without the siren going. The car stops, turns off its engine. Now I can hear car doors being opened and slammed, one after the other, and footsteps on the path outside my house.

There's the bell. Short and sharp. A pause, and then the creak of floorboards downstairs as Mum walks from the kitchen to the front door.

It's happening.

I'm holding my breath.

I hear the sound of low, muffled voices. Mum is crying, quietly at first, then louder and all gaspy, like she can hardly breathe. I can picture it all. I've seen scenes like this on TV shows. They're telling her they think they've found Holly. They're saying someone has to go down to the morgue to identify her. It'll just be a formality, although everyone will be hoping until the last second that it isn't her. But it will be her. And then it will be over. And nothing will ever be the same again.

"Sam! Come down! *Sam!*" Mum is calling me, her voice breaking. "They've found your sister, Sam. Come here now!"

I hesitate. I feel safe in my room. Outside my door is a world I don't want to enter: a world where I'm not a twin or even a brother any more. I drag myself up from my bed, tuck in my shirt and walk slowly to my bedroom door.

And then, impossibly, I hear the sound of my sister's voice. My brain can't compute it at first. It's her, saying, "I'm sorry, so sorry."

And I realize that the gaspy crying is hers, not Mum's. My legs won't work properly, so I peer down from the top of the stairs. It *is* Holly. She seems different somehow: smaller, older. Much more than fifteen minutes older than me.

She looks up at me, her eyes filled with tears, and she nods.

"All right, Sam?" she says.

"All right?"

It's Never Really Super Being Sub

(Sam Cohen's poem)

I've trained just the same
For every single game
But I'm on the bench again
It's never really super being sub

The practice has been fine
I've put in the same time
But I'm always twelfth in line
It's never really super being sub

I know my job and understand
Listened to the game plan
But I'm still the last man
It's never really super being sub

Squad player – that's me
Waiting here patiently
For my opportunity
It's never really super being sub

One chance – all I ask
I know I'm up to the task
It's a test I know I'll pass
It's never really super being sub

A CLEAN SHEET

VINCENT KOMPANY

The bus jolted to a stop. Olly looked up
from his football magazine. The driver
was waving his arms at a car in front.
No surprise there. On most rides to school
this bus driver had an argument with
somebody somewhere along the route.

Olly leant back in his seat and turned the page. Great: another interview with Cristiano Ronaldo. I mean, so what? Who cares what Cristiano has for breakfast? Why wasn't there ever anything about Shelby Town? Olly was just thinking he might write in to the magazine to complain when...

"Oooowwww!"

A big, strong whiff of salt and vinegar crisps came wafting round the side of Olly's head and something grabbed his ear; it felt like a pair of pliers that was being twisted, hard.

"Ooowwww!"

Without even looking, Olly knew who it was. Everybody at school knew that smell. That's why Frankie Brooks's nickname was "Crisps". Frankie was the biggest bully in Year 8 and he had the smelliest breath, too. And the only good thing about that  was it meant you could usually smell Frankie Brooks coming. Except for this morning, when Olly had been too busy wondering about other things to notice. And now Brooks was sitting behind him, with a handful of Olly's ear.

"All right, Olly?" Crisps said. "What's in your comic?"

"I dunno. Cristiano Ronaldo. Would you mind letting go?"

Incredibly, that was exactly what Frankie Brooks did.

"Oh, yeah," he grunted. "I was only trying to get your attention. Budge up. Let me sit down."

Before Olly had the chance to argue – not that he would have anyway – Frankie had squeezed in alongside him. Olly noticed that the low buzz of conversation on the bus had stopped. He could hear the bus creaking as it went round the  corner onto the High Street. And he could hear himself creaking too, as he squirmed in his seat, pushing himself up as tight against the window as he could.

Brooks slowly prised the magazine out of Olly's hand and started flicking through the pages.

"Well done yesterday, Olly. Suppose you're one of us now."

"One of who, Frankie?"

"Us, Olly. Us. You saw me set off that fire extinguisher outside Mr Foster's office yesterday. And you never said a word, did you? I like that. Bit of loyalty. No grassing. You should come and hang about with us lot at lunchtime. We have a right laugh most days, you know."

Olly swallowed hard. It sounded like Frankie was trying to be friendly. Which was almost as scary as him being a bully.

"Um, thanks. But I play football at lunchtime. Well, and at break, too. Any time I can, really."

"Oh, yeah. That's right. You're the one who thinks he's going to end up playing for Shelby Town, aren't you? Fat chance. You'd do better to stick with me, Olly. Pays to know who your friends are, doesn't it? And, you know, anyone who isn't my friend *must* be my enemy."

"No, no. I just..." Olly's voice tailed off. He was a bit stuck here. What would it be? Days on end of ducking and diving, with the smell of salt and vinegar crisps waiting for him around every corner? Or break times spent agreeing with everything Frankie said, like the

159

rest of the gang did? And laughing whenever Frankie found somebody to pick on.

"So, think about it, Olly," whispered Frankie. "See you at lunchtime, eh?"

And with that, Crisps got up and walked off towards his seat at the back of the bus, taking Olly's football magazine with him. Olly's eyes stung and his cheeks burned. One of "Us"? Or one of "Them"? He didn't really want to be either. He just wanted to play football.

Half an hour later, Olly was in a line of excited boys waiting outside the hall. But Olly wasn't excited. In fact, he had a sick feeling in the pit of his stomach. His chat with his new "mate" on the bus had ruined the morning. A morning he'd really been looking forward to.

A whisper crept along the line. "He's here!"

The doors of the hall opened, and in a flash Olly had got himself a seat right in the front row. It wasn't only down the right wing that a turn of pace came in handy. No sooner had everybody got themselves settled than the doors swung open again. A ripple of applause started to break out in the back rows. By the time it hit the front ones, that ripple had become a roar: it sounded like five to three on a Saturday, when the players ran out for a game at Manor Park.

And there he stood, about three metres away from Olly: the Shelby Town striker, Tom Allenby. The head, Mrs Howard, was leading him to the front of the hall. He was wearing his Town tracksuit, a shiny new pair of trainers and a big, wide smile. Olly stared, open-mouthed. It was the first time he'd ever seen a real player up close. The clapping died down and Mrs Howard, who'd gone all red and a bit girly-looking, introduced their special guest.

"Hi boys," said Tom. "Mrs Howard wanted me to speak to you about my time at school as well as about my life as a footballer. To be honest, I'm not all that good at making speeches. I leave them to our manager, Dave Morgan. So how about you just ask me questions?"

Hands went up all over the hall. Over the next half an hour, Tom Allenby did his best to answer everyone: *Will Town stay up again next season? Who's the best player you've ever played against? Who's the worst-dressed player at the club? How much money do you make a week? What car do you drive? What did you think of England at the World Cup? How did you become a player? How can I become a player?*

It could have gone on like that for the rest of the day. In fact, Olly was sure he heard a couple of

questions being asked for the second time. But Tom
Allenby was polite and friendly and didn't seem in
a rush to get away. Olly was listening to every word.
Or trying to, anyway, when he wasn't worrying about
what he was going to do at lunchtime.

Finally there was a lull in the questioning and
Mrs Howard cleared her throat.

"Now then, boys. Mr Allenby's answered a lot
of questions already and it's almost time for you
to go back to your lessons. We've heard a lot about
football. Does anyone have anything they want to ask
Mr Allenby about school?"

A hush descended on the hall, and there was a bit
of foot-shuffling. Then a long sigh. Was that Frankie
Brooks letting people know what he thought of school?
Without thinking, Olly stuck his hand in the air.

Tom Allenby looked at him.

"Yes, mate?"

Mrs Howard looked at him.
"Yes, Olly?"

All the other boys in the hall
looked at him too.

Olly gulped. "Mr Allenby …
um … Tom? Um, what was your
best thing about school? And
what was your worst?"

There was a bit of sniggering going on now. Was that Frankie Brooks too? Olly almost wished he hadn't asked, but everyone shut up as soon as Tom Allenby spoke.

"Funny you should ask me that, Olly. Because the best thing and the worst thing at school for me were actually the *same* thing. And that was getting chucked out."

There were one or two giggles. And a few whispers. Mrs Howard looked a bit shocked and then did that funny smile-that-wasn't-a-smile thing she did at parents' evenings.

Olly's eyes widened. "What happened?" he asked.

Tom Allenby glanced at his watch and then across at Mrs Howard. Luckily, right at that moment, Mrs Howard was distracted by a bit of pushing and shoving going on in Frankie Brooks's row towards the back of the hall.

"Brooks! I'll see you later in my office, please!" she said, giving Tom Allenby the chance to start telling Olly his story.

●   ●   ●

"Well," Tom said, "by the time I went to secondary school, all I was interested in was sport. I got my work done but I couldn't wait to be out playing something. Football, of course. But cricket and hockey and athletics as well.

"When I was thirteen, we moved house and so I started at a new school. We had a trip at the end of my first term, kind of a sports weekend. We all stayed in lodges at the edge of some woods and there were playing fields there too. I loved it, of course, and when it came to races or matches, I ended up winning every time.

"On the second day, we did a cross-country race and I came in first with another boy, Brendan. We were miles ahead of anyone else. I hardly ever talked to Brendan. To be honest, he was the kind of lad you steered clear of, really. Always in trouble, always getting into fights and giving teachers lip.

"I was thirsty after the run and the next thing, Brendan said, 'Look. There's a load of orange juices on the back seat of that car.' And before I could say anything, he'd opened the door and helped himself. He threw a carton over to me and, well, like I said, I *was* thirsty. But you can guess what happened next. Out of nowhere, our PE teacher turned up. And he wasn't happy when he saw what we'd done.

"Me and Brendan both got a proper telling-off, in front of everybody. Nothing like that had ever happened to me before. I remember going red and feeling angry because I thought I was being made to look stupid. Anyway, it didn't stop there. That evening, we went out on an adventure thing: torches, maps, clues and all that. It was fun, and my team managed to get back in one piece.

"Later that night, though, a rumour went round that one boy had been in a fight while we were out and got a black eye, and in the morning, the PE teacher came looking for me. I don't know how or why, but he said he knew that I'd been the one who'd given this boy a whack. Of course, I said I didn't know anything about it. Even though I did, really. By then, everybody knew it was Brendan. He'd been showing off about it at breakfast. I wasn't going to say anything, though."

Just at that moment, Mrs Howard clapped her hands. "All right, boys. I think we've taken up enough of Mr Allenby's time."

Olly looked at Tom. And Tom was looking at Mrs Howard. Olly thought she'd been a bit rude, stopping him in the middle of the story. Tom shrugged it off, however, and started signing the bits of paper that boys were sticking under his nose. As the last few boys were drifting away, Olly saw his moment and walked up to Tom. The teachers were already outside the hall, making sure everyone got off to the right classes.

"Excuse me, Mr Allenby," said Olly. "You said it was the worst thing *and* the best thing. Why did you get chucked out of school?"

Tom smiled and sat down in the row where Olly had been sitting.

"Well, Olly, if you're really interested. The teachers couldn't prove anything, but they still thought it was me who'd had the fight. Maybe it was because I was one of the biggest boys in the year. Or because I was new. Anyway, when it came to giving out medals at the end of the trip, they didn't give me one – not one! – even though I'd won all the races and every game we'd played.

"And from then on, at that school, it didn't matter what I said or did. It always seemed like they were looking to blame me for anything bad that happened. To be honest, after a while, they were right to blame me. They treated me like I was a troublemaker, and so I suppose I became one. And do you know what? I even started hanging about with Brendan. He liked that I hadn't told on him. Respected me, I think. And that made me feel good. So I started hanging about with him – and getting into trouble with him, too. There was a little group of us who all the other boys were a bit scared of.

"I kept on with football, of course, but everything else at school got worse and worse. It felt like the teachers really had it in for me, the headmaster especially. I felt like they were looking for an excuse to really teach me a lesson. And football ended up being that excuse. The next year, at half-term, I went away on a football trip with my Saturday morning team. There was a strike at the airport in Spain and we were late getting back. I missed two days of school.

"Even though my mum wrote to explain what had happened, I got called into the headmaster's office and he ripped into me: *You should have told us where you were going. You shouldn't even have gone. You should have done such and such.* He just went on and on. I could have argued back but I just thought it was better to stand there and take it. And I thought that would be it. But I was wrong, Olly. Completely wrong.

"At the end of term, when my report came home, none of the teachers had written anything about my subjects. There was nothing on the report except a long note from the headmaster at the end. I thought that was strange. So did my mum and dad. But the strangest thing was that the writing was so bad, we couldn't work out what it said. Dad said not to worry.

We could ask about it when I went back in September.

"To be honest, I'd completely forgotten about it by the time school started again. I had other things to worry about. I broke my ankle during the holidays and had to have my foot put in plaster. They said it would be six months, probably, before I could play football again. Which was like a death sentence for me. After the holidays, I just went back into school as normal. Well, except I was hobbling and really fed up.

"After a couple of days, I got a message to say that the head wanted to see me. I limped along to his office and he asked me what I was doing there. 'Didn't you read your report?' he said. I thought I'd be in even more trouble if I said I couldn't read his writing. So I just looked at the floor. And he went on about how I was no longer welcome at the school, what did I think I was playing at coming back here. 'You've been making too much trouble,' he finished.

"I couldn't believe it. But, at the same time, I wasn't really surprised. Dad wanted to go up to the school but Mum stopped him. She said she would find out about other schools and then we'd decide what to do next. I stayed home for a couple of days and got bored pretty quickly. Nobody from school got in touch – not even Brendan and the other boys I thought were my mates.

"In the end, Mum sorted things out. Like she

always did. I ended up going to a school that was much further from home but actually closer to the football club where I trained. I could walk there at the end of lessons. At first, I thought the other kids at the school were trying to avoid me. And that the teachers were looking at me as if they expected me to do something wrong. I didn't really know what to do. Or to say. So I just got on with my work and looked forward to playing football again.

"It didn't take long before I started to make friends. There was one boy who played at the same club as me, and he sort of looked out for me. I didn't need to act tough, like I had when I was in Brendan's little gang. And that meant that the teachers didn't seem to pick on me like they had at my old school. I could just be me. Do what I had to do and get off to play football.

"Getting chucked out of school was horrible, but things came out right. I didn't have to be the person I'd been before. I could just be who I wanted to be. It was as if that new school was a clean sheet for me and I could start all over again. I could be who I wanted to be instead of who people expected me to be."

Olly stared at Tom Allenby. He could hardly believe the story. Today of all days.

"Are you all right, Olly?" Tom asked.

"Yeah," stuttered Olly. "It's just…"

Just then, Mrs Howard's voice rang out from the back of the hall.

"Oliver! What are you doing? You should be in class with everyone else."

Before Olly could answer, Tom stood up. "Sorry, Mrs Howard. My fault. I just wanted to ask Olly about his football and what he thought of Shelby Town."

"Oh," replied Mrs Howard. "Oh, well, that's all right then, I suppose. But come on, Oliver. Get your bag and come along now." She walked back out into the corridor.

"Thanks, Mr Allenby," said Olly.

"That's all right, Olly." Tom laughed. "Couldn't have you getting in trouble for listening to me, could I?"

"No, no. Not that," Olly said. "I meant thanks for the story."

The Town striker looked at Olly. Olly was about to explain why Tom's story had meant so much to him; tell him everything that had happened that morning. But Mrs Howard's voice boomed out again. "Oliver!"

Olly put out his hand. Tom shook it and smiled. "Good to meet you, Olly."

"Good to meet you, too, Mr Allenby."

Olly's lessons seemed to fly past that morning and suddenly it was lunchtime. Olly hurried out into the

playground after double science, expecting the smell
of crisps to hit him as soon as he stepped outside. But
there was no sign of Frankie Brooks. Olly reached
into his bag and pulled out his tennis ball. Some of
the boys were already waiting for him down by the
wall with the goal painted on it. Olly kicked the ball
towards them and ran after it.

Within a couple of minutes, he was swept up in the
game. It was his form against the boys from Year 9.
Olly was playing a blinder. It was as if that tennis
ball was stuck to his foot.

The keeper, a kid named
Dan Hammond, rolled the
ball to him and Olly
was away down
the right wing.
None of the older boys
could keep up. Then,
just at that moment,
out of the corner of his
eye, Olly saw Frankie
Brooks coming down
the steps into the playground.

Olly stopped kicking the ball and thought about
the conversation they'd had on the bus. Then he
remembered what Tom Allenby had said about being

who he wanted to be. For Olly, that meant imagining
he was playing in front of 30,000 people at Manor
Park. He took a deep breath and kept running.

There was only one defender between him and
the goal. As he came out to close him down,
Olly checked inside and shot with
the outside of his right foot.

The ball flew past the keeper and hit the wall so hard, it bounced all the way back to Dan in the opposite goal. All his mates jumped on top of him.

"Goal of the day, Olly! Goal of the month!"

Olly's grinning face poked out from the midst of the huddle of bodies. Frankie Brooks was looking straight at him, half sneering. But he was speechless for once – even he had to admit it had been *some* goal. All of a sudden, Olly had that sick feeling in his stomach again. But Frankie Brooks wasn't going to stop him making his own mind up about what to do next. Carry on playing? Go and hang out with Crisps? Go and find a teacher to tell?

No. Olly looked straight back across the playground and shouted out, "Come on, Frankie. Come and join us. Don't you fancy a game?"

BEEN THERE, DONE THAT

(Tom Allenby's poem)

There's nothing really new
I've seen it all before
Matches, players, managers
You bet I know the score
There's nothing you can tell me – I know where it's at
Got the T-shirt, mate – been there, done that

Windy Wednesday nights away
Winters wild and wet
The crowd – one man and his dog
The best you're going to get
Changing rooms like caravans – no room to swing a cat
Got the T-shirt, pal – been there, done that

I've had it tough and had it rough
You don't hear me complaining
The football school of hard knocks
Is where I've done my training
Experience? It's all up here – don't need to see no stats
Got the T-shirt, buddy – been there, done that

Football isn't rocket science
Just plain old common sense
Keep the ball, score a goal
Solid in defence
Do your job, safety first — and don't give me no chat
Got the T-shirt, son — been there, done that

THE FINAL WHISTLE

TERRY DEARY

Monday lunchtime

Ellie Dodds said, "Your grandfather
is a liar." She didn't say it quite like
that. She was prodding me in the
shoulder with a finger as fat as a
prime pork sausage. "Your" – *prod*
– "grandfather" – *prod* – "is"
– *prod* – "a" – *prod* –
"li-" – *prod* – "ar."

We were in the school yard and half the school had gathered round to watch. Her face was close to mine. I noticed she had a spot on the side of her nose that turned redder as she grew angry.

"What is your grandfather, Billy?"

"My grandfather is my father's father," I said and tried to look stupid, not cheeky. If she thought I was making fun of her, I'd have had five prime pork sausages rolled into a fist and planted on my nose.

You could tell the rest of the kids were just waiting for it. Nothing like a bit of blood on the playground, is there? I like to watch it myself. Just not when it's my blood.

"Fight," someone muttered and the words spread around the circle of eager faces. I prayed for the whistle to signal the end of break.

Ellie Dodds's face turned as red as the spot on her nose while the spot itself turned purple. "Repeat after me, Billy Campbell: My grandfather is a liar…"

"Um…"

No whistle. No sign of Mr Golden Eagle Arthurton with his beaky nose. When I was in junior school, I used to think teachers cut our breaks as short as they could. They wanted to rush us back to the classrooms. When I got to secondary, I found the teachers wanted the world's longest fifteen-minute breaks, in no rush to get back to class. They hate us as much as we hate them.

So, no whistle.

"Repeat after me, Billy Campbell: My grandfather is a liar…"

"Yes, Ellie," I said boldly, "your grandfather is a liar."

Now her face turned purple and the spot seemed to be throbbing a yellow light. I couldn't take my eyes off it. I was sure it was going to explode.

"Fight!" someone shouted and stamped his foot like a drum. "Fight," the word echoed and the feet rumbled on the tarred yard.

The sausages were raised and ready to strike. I closed my eyes and waited.

Ah, you think I should have fought back, do you? Well you never met Ellie Dodds. Let her punch you and she walks away happy. Fight back and she punches you twenty times more.

Or maybe you think I should have just said, "My granddad is a liar"?

I'd rather be punched a hundred and twenty times, thanks.

I half opened my eyes again. I saw the fat fist pulled back.

The whistle went for the end of break. The crowd of kids let out a sigh. "Awwww!" Disappointed.

"I'll get you after school, tomorrow, Billy Campbell," Ellie said, dropping her fist. "Tonight I'm off to a meeting of the Shelby Town Supporter's Club. My Dad is the President, you know."

Yes, I knew.

"I'm playing football tomorrow night," I told her. "For the school team. Last game of the season … we only need a draw to win the league."

"Ooooh," she sneered. "Surprised you aren't playing for Shelby Town. Like your lying granddad."

I walked towards the main door into the school and Ellie followed. The Golden Eagle glared at both of us. Ellie smiled at him as sweetly as she knew how. That's about as sweet as a bottle of vinegar.

"You'll be playing with a broken leg," she hissed, and vanished into the sour-smelling gloom of the school.

"Last game of the season," I repeated, calling after her. "Will you break my leg before the game or after?"

"After."

"You could come along and watch," I said, muttering under my breath, "if you're not too busy pulling the legs off spiders or bullying boys that are smaller than you."

She stopped. Her face was pale now in the dim

corridor. That was even scarier than her angry face. "I'll be there," she promised. "Maybe I'll break both your legs."

Monday afternoon

I sighed. It was all my fault. I had been so pleased that morning. So-o-o-o pleased. I had stood up in assembly to tell everyone about my famous granddad.

Now, at the end of the school day, I trudged home with my backpack full of homework. Other students walked along in little groups. No one walked with me. Not after lunch ... and what Ellie Dodds had told everyone.

I turned up our street – a row of terraced houses – and saw the nurse's car outside our door. I walked into the house and it smelt like a hospital. The door was open to the downstairs bedroom and the nurse was wittering. "Now, Jack, that's your nappy changed. You'll be comfy till I get back in the morning, won't you?"

Granddad didn't reply. He lay in the bed, mouth open and twisted down to one side. His grey eyes were as pale and watery as Shelby Town tea. The nurse looked up and saw me. "There you are, Billy. Just in time to take over."

"Yes, but I wanted to ask—"

"Your dad said he'd be home in an hour. You can manage till then, can't you?"

"Yes, but—"

"And remember what I said yesterday? Your granddad has had a stroke. He needs to get his brain working again. Sometimes they lose their memory, you know. It's up to you to talk to him – keep his memories fresh. It'll all help," she said as she packed her bag and put on her coat.

Then she was gone. Granddad turned his eyes towards me. He struggled to make the words come out. "Hello, our Jim," he finally managed.

"Billy," I told him. "I'm not Jim … I'm Billy."

He frowned. "I don't know any Billy."

"I'm your grandson," I reminded him.

"Are you?"

His eyes fixed on my scarf. "Shelby Town, eh?" he said and saliva dribbled down his chin. "I used to play for Shelby Town, you know."

I sighed. Here we go again. It was going to be a long hour till Dad got home.

Monday evening

"You didn't play for Shelby Town, Granddad," I said quietly.

"Not…" He struggled to find the word. "Not lately."

I wanted to say "Not ever", but I hadn't the heart. If he wanted to think he was a football star, then let him. He'd been living with Dad and me for a month and hadn't said anything about football before. He'd been poorly, had no one to care for him, and so Dad said he was coming to live with us. "Just till he gets better," Dad explained.

But after two weeks he got worse.

I hadn't met my granddad before – well, not since I was a baby, he said. And I didn't remember that, of course. He lived in Scotland. A quiet and shy sort of man, so we hadn't had much to say to each other after he moved in. Not until he turned really ill.

I got back from school after a game one night and found him lying on the floor in front of the fire. I thought he was dead.

Well, I would think that. I've never seen a dead person, have you? I mean, I knew about death. My mum died when I was born and Dad brought me up. But I'd never seen death close up.

My mouth was dry and my legs didn't want to move. It was all I could do to find my mobile in my pocket. My hands were shaking so much, I could hardly punch in 999.

Then I heard a croak, a groan like an old door, and I saw the fingers on his left hand twitch. The ambulance was there in five minutes and I don't think I'd moved.

After a week in hospital they sent him back to our house. That's when the nurse explained about his memory. "Get him to talk about the past," she advised.

And that's where all the trouble had started.

1973

"Remember 1973, Jim?" asked Granddad.

"Billy," I corrected.

"I played for Shelby for five years – '70 to '75," he went on softly.

I remembered Ellie Dodds's words. I said nothing.

"Back in those days they were non-league. They're in the Second Division now, of course..."

"The Premier League," I said.

He turned his eyes towards me. Seeing me as if for the first time. "What's that?"

"Nothing, Granddad."

"Non-league, we were … but we caused the biggest upset in cup history," he said. The left side of his face was not frozen by the stroke. It crinkled a little in a smile. "A non-league side got all the way to the third round of the FA Cup. The whole town was excited. The ground only held five thousand, but fifty thousand wanted to see us play in that third round ... that's when the First Division teams joined the cup, of course."

I nodded. It was going to be the same story he'd told me the night before. The long lie. I looked out of the window, through the faded net curtains, into the April evening. And let him get on with it.

"You were there, Jim, weren't you? You were there, son? For the West Ham cup match?"

"Yes, Granddad," I sighed. I wasn't born. It was useless to say.

"Shelby drew First Division West Ham. Their top scorer was "Pop" Robson – Bryan Robson was his real name – a little feller from Sunderland. They called him Pop because he looked older than his years – the Bald Assassin. Top goal-scorer in the First Division. And he was coming to Shelby."

"Yes, Granddad."

"What a day – the greatest day of my life."

I was suddenly sad. This old man remembering his greatest day ... a day that never happened.

"I'd hurt a hamstring," my granddad said. "I hadn't played for a month so I was on the sidelines for that game. The crowd was spilling onto the pitch and they let an old bloke sit next to me on the bench. Hah! Wouldn't happen these days, would it, Jim?"

I shook my head. The old man's eyes were glowing in the dim evening light. "You're a good player, they tell me, Jim. Wish I could get to see you play. Just once. Too busy. I'd like to see you play."

"Tell me about West Ham, Granddad," I suggested.

"That Pop Robson was a different class. Fast feet, that was his secret. He turned us inside out. Twenty minutes gone and we were two down. The crowd had gone a bit quiet. They expected us to lose ... but not roll over and die so easily. I was holding my head in my hands and the old bloke next to me said, 'It isn't over till the final whistle, Jack.' I thought he was dreaming, of course. And what happened next?"

"Shelby scored, Granddad." It was the same story he'd told the night before. The one I'd repeated in assembly this morning.

"Aye. Shelby scored. I'm forgetting, you were there, Jim."

"No, Granddad."

"Then, on the half-hour, that Pop Robson put his bald head on the ball and thumped it past our keeper: 3–1 and I was sure we wouldn't come back a second time. But that old feller just laughed and said, 'It isn't over till the final whistle, Jack.'

And then he said, 'If you were on the pitch you could make a difference … your pace on the wing's what Shelby needs.' And, blow me, what happened?"

"Shelby's fullback got injured and you went on."

He tried to nod but his head wouldn't move. He licked his lips and I wiped a wet sponge over his tongue. "I never knew who that old bloke was … he wasn't there when the game ended and I never saw him again. Sometimes I think … I think he was a ghost. Aye, that's daft, I know. But I went on as a sub and it was like I was electric. I started to run at their defence and beat those Hammers defenders like they weren't there. They were glad to hear the half-time whistle, I can tell you. And the crowd … the crowd that had gone quiet … roared us off. 3–1 down but not out."

"It isn't over till the final whistle," I said.

"The second half … it's still talked about at Shelby today, I bet. We kicked off … the ball came out to me … I raced down the wing and crossed and Eddie Paynton nodded it in to make it 3–2. West Ham weren't attacking any more. Even Pop Robson was helping out in defence. They packed their box. We couldn't get through. Then with ten minutes to go they got so desperate, they fouled Eddie. Penalty."

"And you took it, Granddad."

"Aye, I'm forgetting you were there, Jim. I never

thought I'd miss. And I didn't. Nearly burst the net, son. 3–3 and ten minutes to go. Ten minutes to make history… Five minutes to go and the Bald Assassin hit our crossbar. I guess that woke us up. Our keeper collected it and threw it out to me on the right wing. I was just inside our half. There was only one place I was heading."

"Towards their goal," I put in.

"Aye. They'd just been attacking. They were tired. Slow to get back. Shelby Town were tired too, but I'd only played fifty minutes. I put my head down and ran down the wing. I'd gone round the outside of their fullback half a dozen times that afternoon, so he moved over to block me. And I did the last thing he expected – I cut inside. Their centre back was still up the field in our half. The goal was open in front of me. I pulled back my left leg and let fly. Top right-hand corner. Their keeper never had a chance."

Granddad's eyes began to close and his voice was a whisper. "The crowd were on the pitch. We were winning 4–3 with a minute to go. The pitch was cleared but the ref would add on time. I told my mates to be careful. 'It isn't over till the final whistle,' I said. But we hung on. Till…"

"The final whistle," I finished. But Granddad didn't hear me. He was asleep.

Tuesday afternoon

On that day back in '73, when Shelby knocked West
Ham out of the cup, my granddad was the hero. That
was the story I'd told the whole school on Monday
morning.

Then, Monday lunchtime, Ellie Dodds had come
up to me and said, "Liar. I phoned my Dad ... he's
president of the Shelby Town Supporter's Club. Nobody
called Campbell has ever played for Shelby. He checked
the record books. And there was no Campbell in the
famous 1973 team. Your granddad is a liar."

And that's when she poked me and said she'd
break my legs.

After school today I was in the dressing room and
then out onto the pitch before Ellie could get me. She
had a detention.

Let me ask you something. Do you believe in
ghosts? Granddad reckoned the old bloke on the Shelby
bench may have been a ghost. I've read books about
spirits. They say that a person dies and then appears
to the living just once on their way to the afterlife.

Is it true? I don't know. But listen to my story and
make up your own mind.

We kicked off at quarter past four. After half an
hour we were pressing. Our goalkeeper bowled the ball
to me on the right wing. I ran at their fullback and

suddenly remembered what my granddad had told me. *"I cut inside… The goal was open in front of me."*

I cut inside.

That's when it turned weird. It seemed like everyone on the pitch was frozen in time. No one moved towards me. My own team had no one in the penalty area for me to pass to. Even the crowd seemed silent as a winter night. *"I pulled back my left leg and let fly. Top right-hand corner,"* Granddad had said. In that eerie silence I pulled back my left leg … and that's when it all went wrong.

I got my toe under the ball but then caught my studs in the grass, sending a feeble shot looping into the air. Their keeper watched it, yet he seemed to move in slow motion as it sailed over his head. Super-slow motion… The ball dropped behind the keeper, landed on the goal line and bounced gently into the net.

Back to real time and my teammates were shaking my hand and hugging me. I was just stunned. I'd scored – but it was a freak goal. I looked up at the clock on the changing-room roof. Quarter to five.

In the second half we gave away a soft own goal but we hung on to win the league. The teachers and the lads were well chuffed, but all I could think of was Ellie Dodds, waiting by the main gates with a bunch of her friends.

I changed as quickly as I could and ran out of the side gate to dodge them, but they spotted me. I heard Ellie's angry cries and looked back to see five big kids pounding down the road towards me. I was aching from playing ninety minutes and their shouts were getting closer by the time I turned into our street.

I stopped suddenly. There were cars outside our house … the nurse's car and two strange ones. But it was the sight of the ambulance with the lights flashing that stopped the kids who were chasing me. They just gawped, the way people do.

The paramedics carried out a stretcher with a covered shape on it. I jogged down the street. Dad was standing at the door talking to the nurse. When he saw me he tried to smile.

"Granddad?"

"He had another stroke," he said gently. "He died."

"When?" Stupid question. "What time did he die?"

"About a quarter to five."

And I remembered Granddad's words, *"Wish I could get to see you play. Just once. Too busy. I'd like to see you play."* Maybe he had.

But Granddad was a fake, wasn't he? I really needed to know. "Did your dad ever play winger for Shelby Town?" I asked.

Dad snorted. "Don't be daft, Billy. My dad couldn't run from the pub, let alone run down Shelby wing. Why do you ask?"

"He told me he did," I mumbled.

Dad frowned. "My *dad* told you? My dad died before you were born, son."

It was my turn to frown. "So who just died in our downstairs bedroom?"

"Your granddad."

"Your dad?"

"No, no, no. Your mother's dad ... Jack Macdonald."

And suddenly I understood.

Friday and Saturday

It was a busy week. First the stream of reporters knocking on the door, wanting to interview us about the famous Jack Macdonald, hero of the Shelby Cup shock of 1973, who'd moved away to Scotland after he left the club.

You couldn't move in the house for flowers and cards. The lamppost outside was muffled in a hundred scarves and Shelby strips. Kids left their teddy bears and fans left photos and flowers on the doorstep. The little scribbled notes could have caught fire in the rows of candles. Reporters were camped in the street and at our school.

On Wednesday, there was a special assembly where the headmaster reminded everybody that Jack Macdonald was the very same man that Billy Campbell – me – had told them about just a couple of days before. We said prayers for him.

On Thursday Jack's son, Jim, turned up for the funeral. It was the first time I'd met my Uncle Jim.

On Friday it was the funeral. One of the biggest Shelby has ever seen. Hundreds stood outside in the graveyard listening to the service among the television cameras and the newspaper reporters. But it was inside the church that was most amazing.

All the current players from Shelby Town Football Club were there to "pay their respects", plus dozens of the retired players – men who were heroes in our town. But not one of them as great a hero as my granddad. At least, that's what the vicar said.

Of course the President of Shelby Town Supporter's Club was there too, and he managed to get a seat inside the church. Along with his daughter, Ellie Dodds. At the end, Dad and I stood at the door of the church and shook the hands of our heroes. Ellie looked on with envy.

After we left the church I saw her standing by the gate. She raised five pork-sausage fingers in the air in a high-five. I slapped her hand as she said, "Your granddad was a hero, Billy, a hero. Respect. Sorry about ... you know."

She blushed till her spot turned purple.

My granddad, a liar on Monday, was a hero by Friday. "Forget it," I said as if I forgave her. But I'd never forgive her one thing. Because of her, I spent my last hours with my granddad thinking he was a liar.

Saturday was a home game against Sunderland – hometown of the Bald Assassin, Granddad's old enemy. A story went round that Pop Robson was in the crowd. Before kick-off the announcer called for a minute's applause in memory of Jack Macdonald ... my granddad. It rumbled like thunder and shook the tears out of my eyes till they splashed onto the seat in front of me.

Shelby won the game – of course – with a lot of luck. After the final whistle, Dad said, "They reckon ghosts visit their favourite people before they pass on. I guess today was your granddad's final visit."

I shrugged. I didn't think so.

The old footballer had heard another final whistle, another place, another time.

THE ANGELS OF PERU

MAL PEET

Paul Faustino was on a holiday that had turned out to be something else. Work, in fact. He'd been owed leave from his newspaper, *La Nación*. But then, two days before he'd left, his boss – that crocodile, Carmen – had slunk into his office and coiled into the guest chair.

"So, Paul," she said. "What are your plans?"

"Oh, nothing much. I thought I'd redecorate the spare room. Catch up on some reading, stuff like that."

"Liar," Carmen said.

"Pardon?"

"You've booked a flight to Spain, leaving on Sunday."

Paul sighed and swivelled away from his screen. "How'd you know that, Carmen?"

She didn't answer his question but said, "What I was thinking was, seeing as you're going all the way to Europe, you might like to—"

"No," he said firmly.

"You haven't heard my proposal."

"I don't want to," Faustino said. "I won't like it."

"We'll pay your airfares. Business class, of course. And expenses."

Faustino did the arithmetic. Eventually he said, "For what?"

A long piece for the weekend magazine. Interviews with South American footballers playing in Spain and Italy. Talking to them about homesickness, money, cultural differences, the ways football is different. About being magazine celebrities. On the way back, a stopover in London, because Carmen was interested in those identical, baby-faced, nineteen-year-old twins, the so-called "Angels of Peru" who played for Chelsea. Gabriel and Rafael. She couldn't remember their last name. Nor could Faustino, at the time.

But there'd been a hitch. The way his flights were scheduled, the only day he could interview the twins was the first of April. And on that day, Chelsea were playing an evening cup tie against Shelby. At Shelby. After a hectic flurry of phone calls and texts, it was arranged that Faustino would interview the boys after the game, at the hotel in Shelby where the team were staying the night. A complimentary ticket for the game  would be waiting for Faustino.

"Good luck with the Angels," the Chelsea press guy had said. "They don't say much. Except to each other."

So here he was, on the train to Shelby. The incredibly expensive train to Shelby. Faustino watched the suburbs of London pass away behind him. When the trolley came, he asked for a bottle of mineral water (he'd been warned about the coffee) and a slice of fruitcake. He was struggling with its plastic wrapping when someone spoke his name. He looked up.

The man was odd-looking. A young, almost childish face set on an older man's head. Balding, but with a wild halo of greying hair. Deep, dark eyes. A cautious smile. He wore a suit and a white shirt, buttoned up to the neck, but no tie. He spoke in Spanish, politely.

"Forgive me. It *is* Paul Faustino, isn't it?"

"Ah, yes," Faustino admitted reluctantly.

The man's smile widened. He clapped his hands together. "Yes! I knew it. I am a great admirer of yours, Señor Faustino. You are one of the few football writers in South America who knows what he is talking about. I have also read your books, which are very good."

"Thank you."

"I recognized you from your book jackets, and because – only three weeks ago, back home – I saw you on television. Arguing with that idiot from *El Sol*."

The man held out his hand. Faustino shook it.

"Theo Chavez," the stranger said, and glanced at the empty seat facing Faustino. "Would you mind if I joined you?"

Faustino shrugged. "No. Please do."

Chavez sat and folded his arms. He studied Faustino as if he were a particularly interesting item in a museum. Just when Faustino was starting to feel uncomfortable, Chavez said, "How extraordinary to meet you on a train in England. May I ask what brings you here?"

Faustino said, "Well, as a matter of fact—"

But Chavez interrupted him by holding up a hand. "No. Let me guess. You are on your way to Shelby to watch the Chelsea game. The semi-final."

"Yes. How did you know that?"

Now Chavez shrugged. "Why else would anyone be going to Shelby? And I suspect that you are particularly interested in the boys they call the Angels, from Peru. Rafael and Gabriel."

Faustino raised his eyebrows. Chavez smiled again. "Not a very wild guess," he said. "After all, you are a sports writer and the twins have become celebrities back in Peru. And all over South America. You can't walk past a news stand without seeing their faces staring out at you."

Now Faustino had placed the man's accent. "You are from Peru, Señor Chavez?"

"Call me Theo, please. What do you think of those boys? As players, I mean."

"I'm embarrassed to say that I have never seen them play live," Faustino said. They came over here when they were, what, seventeen? But from games

I've seen on TV, I have to say they seem amazingly talented."

Chavez nodded. "Yes. Soon, they will be the two best mid-fielders in the game. Gabriel is the better defender. He reads the opposition very well, sees what they intend to do. He and Ashley Cole are already the best left-side partnership in the world, I think. He is a great passer of the ball from deep positions. But in offence, Rafael is the more inventive player. He is very good at appearing from nowhere and attacking the box. Chelsea let him roam, so there is always confusion about who should be covering him when he comes through. Unfortunately, he has something of a temperament. Eleven yellow cards and two reds this season."

Faustino said, "You obviously follow them with great interest."

"Of course," Chavez said. "They are my sons."

Faustino spluttered mineral water. A little came out of his nose. When he'd recovered his composure, he said "Forgive me, Señor ... er, Theo. Do you mean that literally? That you are Gabriel and Rafael's father?"

"Yes. And I am very happy because I will be with my boys today. I haven't seen them for eleven months and twenty days. Each year my sons send me the money to come to England for a month. I look forward to it very much."

Faustino had a good nose for liars and con artists. In his line of work, he met them on a daily basis. But there was no whiff of dishonesty coming off Theo Chavez. The man's face was almost unnaturally innocent. His happiness and his pride seemed entirely genuine. And there was no mistaking his physical resemblance to the Angels.

"Well," Faustino said. "It's a fantastic coincidence, meeting you like this."

"Perhaps it is fate."

"Yes, perhaps. You know, before I came over I did a bit of homework on Gabriel and Rafael, but I couldn't find anything much in the way of family background. I didn't come across an interview with you, for instance."

"No," Chavez said. "We don't trust journalists."

"Quite right too," Faustino said seriously.

Chavez's smile flickered. "Forgive me, Paul. I didn't mean... You are an exception, of course."

"Thank you," Faustino said graciously. He glanced at his watch. An hour and a quarter before the train got to Shelby.

"Ah, look, Theo, I wonder if you..." Faustino hesitated, tried to look a little ashamed of himself. "I know this is a cheek, but I wonder if you would do me the honour of granting me an interview. I mean, this seems like a God-sent opportunity. My editor would kill me if—"

"An interview? You mean now?"

"Yes. I'll understand if you refuse, of course."

Chavez looked out at the alien green landscape blurring past the window. Faustino waited.

"OK," Chavez said at last.

"Excellent! Thank you."

Faustino stood and rummaged in his bag for his voice recorder. He set it on the table and squinted at its tiny buttons. "You happy to talk to this thing, Theo? We just need to use normal voices. It's very sensitive."

"Sure," Chavez said.

When the machine's green light came on, Faustino said, "So. As I recall, the boys grew up in a place called La Hoya. Up in the mountains, right? What can you tell me about it?"

Chavez grunted, half humorously. "A little place. Rough. Poor. There are only two temperatures up there: hot as hell or cold as ice."

"And may I ask what you did for a living?"

"Auto repair. Me and the boys lived in two rooms over the workshop."

"You and the boys? Was their mother...?"

"May I see your ticket, please, sir?"

A guy in a blue uniform was looking down at Faustino. Faustino sighed and pressed the *pause* button on his recorder. Fished his ticket out of his jacket pocket. The guy printed a smudge on it, thanked him and moved on down the carriage. It was odd that he hadn't asked to see Chavez's ticket, that he hadn't even appeared to notice the Peruvian. But Faustino gave it no thought at the time.

Paul pressed *record* again, and, as if nothing had happened, Chavez continued. "My wife died ten days after the twins were born. The births were hard. They damaged her. We had no hospital in La Hoya."

"I'm very sorry," Faustino said.

"The will of God," Chavez said.

"Yeah. So, you brought the boys up single-handed?"

"No, no. How could I? A father with twin babies? And I had a business to run."

"So…?"

"I had a niece, Dolores. My older sister's eldest daughter. She was seventeen. A beautiful soul but, unfortunately, lacking the physical beauty to go with it. Her mother despaired of her ever finding a husband. So I talked to my sister, and Dolores came to live with us, to look after the boys. She had four younger brothers so she knew what to do. At first they all shared the big bed. Then, when that became … inappropriate, I built myself a little lean-to shack on the side of the workshop and Dolores moved into my old bedroom."

"Sounds like a hard life, Theo," Faustino said. "But the boys did OK?"

"Yes and no, Paul. La Hoya was – is – a backward sort of a place. Superstitious. Identical twins were … how should I say it? *Suspect*. Not normal. Old women would often cross themselves when the boys passed by. And Gabriel and Rafael … well, you know, they played tricks on people. They had ways of communicating with each other that no one else understood, not even myself or Dolores. It was hard for other kids to be friends with them. At the school, the teachers gave up trying to tell them apart. They gave them the same mark for everything and wrote exactly the same things about them in their school reports. The boys thought it was funny."

"Yeah," Faustino said. "I can see how that would work. Almost like having a superpower or something. The ability to be two people at once; to mess with people's heads. Useful on the football pitch, too, I would think."

There were rumours that Chelsea used the twins interchangeably, played Gabriel in Rafael's shirt, and vice versa. Faustino was hoping that Chavez might rise to the bait and say something indiscreet. He didn't.

So Faustino said, "And do you still live in La Hoya, Theo?"

"Oh no. I'm in a much better place now."

Yeah, Faustino thought. The boys would've bought dear old Dad a nice apartment in the Lima suburbs. Maybe with a view of the sea.

Back to the subject. "So, um, the boys played football with the other kids in town, right? And they got noticed?"

Chavez said, "I guess they played with the other kids now and again. But they were loners. I used to worry about it, but..."

He shrugged. Faustino nodded sympathetically, then said, "So when did you realize they were special? In football terms, I mean."

Chavez brightened up again. "That's a question I *can* answer. I remember the day as if it were yesterday. I was in the workshop, underneath a Ford pick-up, seeing if I could figure out a way to make the suspension last another six months. Then I hear Dolores come in, see her legs on the other side of the truck. She says, 'Uncle Theo? You got a minute? I think you oughta come and see what the twins are doin' in the yard.' Now the yard was just a big patch of dirt behind the workshop, where I had wrecks parked for spare parts. Rafael and Gabriel had painted a half-size goalmouth on the wall and they used to kick a ball around out there. Which was fine by me. At least I knew where they were. But I say, 'Hell, Dolores, I'm busy right now. What're they doing that's so special?' And she says, 'You gotta come and look for once.'

"So I crawl out and go with Dolores into the yard. The boys are there with a ball. Not a football, something a bit smaller. Red-and-white striped. No idea where they got it from. They're doing what the Brazilians call freestyle, you know? Like, juggling with it and doing tricks. Me and Dolores sit down on an old back seat ripped out of a Toyota and watch. I don't know if the boys knew we were there or not. They didn't pay us any heed, anyway. But after a couple of minutes my mouth is hanging open and I'm thinking, Oh, my God. Because it was, I don't know, kind of *spooky*, almost. Mainly because they were doing all this stuff with the ball, but not saying anything to each other. They were completely silent. Rafael would balance the ball on his foot, change feet, lob the ball over one of the wrecks; Gabriel would lean back, take the ball on his chest, let it roll down his leg onto his foot, turn, stop, turn back, side-foot a pass off the bonnet of another wreck and Rafael knew exactly where it would fall. He'd play a one-two around an engine block and hit the goal right in the top corner. Then, without a word, they'd start over again.

"I sat there watching for a long time with my mouth open. They were magical. They were deadly serious. As far as they were concerned, those wrecks and bits of scrap were the Brazilian defence. Or the Argentinian defence. After a while, Dolores said, 'I reckon you should talk to Jinky Lopez.'"

Outside the train window the countryside was giving way to brick suburbs. Faustino said, "Who was Jinky Lopez?"

"He ran a football team in the nearest city, San Miguel. But he had a house in La Hoya. I looked after his car. He was a sort of scout for the big teams."

"Ah, yes," Faustino said, remembering. "San Miguel. Your sons signed for FC San Miguel when they were, what? Fourteen?"

"Yes," Chavez said.

"Then a year later they were recruited by Club Alianza in Lima. Enrolled in their youth academy."

"Yes."

"You sound less than happy about it."

"I was glad for my boys, but I was lost without them. Twice a week I went down to the post office and talked to them on the telephone. By then they were already a little bit famous. People slapped me on the back, congratulated me, you know? Then I would go home to Dolores, who cried a lot because she missed them. And because she had got very fat and grown a moustache. Then one day I was on the phone to Rafael and he told me that he and Gabriel had been given the chance of a lifetime. That a man from England had come to sign them for the great English club Chelsea. My heart died in my chest but I said, 'And what? Are you going?' And he said, 'Yes, Papa. We are going.'"

By the time the train pulled into Shelby, Faustino was feeling pleased with himself. He was pretty sure that his magazine could splatter "EXCLUSIVE" above his interview with Theo Chavez. Spliced with whatever he got from Rafael and Gabriel, it should make a very nice piece. It was even possible that Carmen would show her teeth by way of a smile for once. He parted company with Theo on the station forecourt. Chavez was going, he said, straight to the stadium; Faustino to check into his hotel. He watched the Peruvian melt into the crowd and then headed for the taxi rank.

The game was a good one. Shelby had a highly disciplined defence, which broke up Chelsea's attacks, forcing the visitors to rely on crosses from wide positions. They counter-attacked well too. Twenty minutes in, John Terry had to hoof the ball out of his own goalmouth with his keeper, Čech, sprawled on the six-yard line. But, as great sides always do, Chelsea grabbed the lead just before half-time, and it was Rafael who scored, sneaking into the box to side-foot the ball home from close range.

During the interval, Faustino craned his neck to see if he could spot Theo Chavez in his guest of honour seat in the directors' box, but his view was blocked.

Chelsea scored again early in the second half, and Shelby looked dead and buried. With thirty minutes left to play, the Chelsea manager decided to beef up his defence and substituted Rafael with Gabriel.

The changeover was slightly weird, Faustino thought. It was almost as if Rafael went over to the touchline, did a double hand-slap with himself in a mirror, then ran back onto the pitch.

Just as the game moved into extra time, Gabriel scored Chelsea's third: a free kick from twenty-five yards out that swerved and dipped into the top right-hand corner of the Shelby goal. All in all, Faustino thought, the perfect reunion between Theo and his boys. Nice.

The interview with the twins took place in a private dining room at the Shelby Sheraton Hotel. After the handshakes, the boys sat down, close together, and smiled across the table, recognizing the bafflement on Faustino's face.

"I'm Rafael," the one on the left said.

"I'm Gabriel," the one on the right said.

"OK," Faustino said. "Thanks. And thanks for taking the time to talk to me."

"You're welcome," the twins said, at the same time.

"First thing I have to say is, congratulations. You both played brilliantly this evening."

"Thank you," Gabriel said. "God was with us today."

"Yeah, I guess," Faustino said. "So, as I think

you know, I'd like to talk to you about living and playing in England, the cultural differences, that kind of thing. But first, if you don't mind, I'd like to ask you about what it was like for you guys growing up in La Hoya, being raised by your cousin … um … Dolores. Your training sessions in the back yard, stuff like that. OK?"

The smiles vanished from the twins' faces. They looked at each other, one frown the reflection of the other. Eventually, Rafael said, "How do you know these things, Señor Faustino? About Dolores and so on? We have never spoken about them."

Faustino grinned, enjoying the moment. "Your father told me. I found it all fascinating, I must say."

Another exchange of glances between the boys.

"You talked with our father?"

"Yes. Didn't he mention it?"

A silence.

Then Gabriel said, "When was this?"

"This afternoon. On the train from London. I'm surprised he…" Faustino's voice trailed off. It was as if the two boys had put on wooden masks. Identical wooden masks. What the hell is going on here? he wondered. What's wrong?

"Is this your idea of a joke, Señor Faustino?"

"What? No. Why do you…?"

Rafael said, "Our father is dead. He died a little less than a year ago."

"What?"

Faustino had the peculiar feeling that the floor had dropped away, and that he and his chair were suspended in space.

"But," he stammered, "I... Wait." He fiddled shakily with his voice recorder. "Please listen to this," he said, pressing the *play* button.

For ten awful seconds, the three of them listened to ... nothing. Nothing other than the muted rush and rumble of a moving train.

Faustino swore and stabbed *forward*. Then *play* again.

Nothing. Not a word.

Faustino sat staring down at the machine for a long moment. When he found the courage to lift his head, the Angels of Peru were gazing at him. The gentle smiles had returned to their faces, and now their eyes were full of forgiveness.

Or was it pity?

Playing at Home, a Long Way from Home

(Dotun Odegbame's poem)

The weather is cold, unfriendly
Everything seems alien
I'm playing at home, a long way from home

I can't understand the manager's jokes
But he smiles, I think he likes me

The lads all laugh, I'm not sure why
But they make me feel welcome

Not sure about chips and lager
Miss my mother's cooking
I'm playing at home, a long way from home

The crowd have now learned my name
Some pronounce it properly

Once they chanted it for two minutes
When I scored my first goal

Don't understand all the words
But football's an international language
Things are getting better, playing at home

Still a very long way from home

BURY AWAY

ALAN DAVIES

If I'd told them once, I'd told them
a hundred times: "Don't be late,
or we'll miss the kick-off." But
getting my mates organized,
as my sister's boyfriend Dave says,
"is like herding cats". This is ironic,
as when it comes to time-keeping,
Dave is the most unreliable of all
the boyfriends she's had.

Anyway, Dave wasn't coming on this trip. He's a born and bred Geordie so he's a Newcastle fan, even though he's lived in Shelby half his life. He comes from Wallsend in Newcastle, which is where Hadrian's Wall ends, or used to end. Josie, my sister, is always on at him to change teams, although she knows perfectly well you can't. Dave just laughs, but it drives me mad every time she starts.

"What? You're not allowed to?" she said on this occasion.

"It's not that you're not allowed to," I said, rising to it already.

"Is it against Premier League rules? You can't change teams?"

"No, it's nothing to do with the rules."

"What about in the transfer window? Can you change then?"

She knew it would wind me up.

"You literally cannot change teams," I told her. "And when I say literally, I mean *literally*. You CAN NOT change. If you love your team, you're stuck with them. And if you're Shelby, you're Shelby till you die and that's it. You wouldn't be able to change even if you wanted to."

"What if Shelby was taken over by a Russian billionaire and he changed the name to Ivan Athletic and moved them to London to play at the Olympic Stadium. Then what?" she persisted. "Still Shelby till you die?"

"That's not going to happen."

She knows this worries me. Ever since that massive Russian bloke was seen being helped out of a limousine outside Manor Park on the day we played Man City.

"You don't know that for sure." She grinned cheekily. "Apparently the Massive Russian was seen in the Hen & Chickens last week. *And* he was at the glove factory the week before. We all saw him when we were on a break. We reckon he's looking to buy it."

"He wasn't at the pub *or* the glove factory!" I exclaimed. "And there's no way he's going to buy the factory. They already have perfectly good gloves in Russia. Where it's freezing."

"They're not lovingly crafted by me and Bea Scanlon, though, are they?" she laughed.

There was no way I was carrying on this conversation. "Go away. I have to go and meet the lads."

"Why don't they come round to you?" asked Josie. "You're driving them all the way up there after all."

"Because," I retorted, "they'll stand around the kitchen gawping at you and we'll never leave."

It was true. My mates never stop going on about Josie. "Where's your skin and blister?" they say, every time I see them. I suppose she is quite pretty, but it's hard to see your sister in that way. She's the one who tells on you to your mum and dad. And even though she's eighteen now and I'm twenty, in some ways it still feels like we're kids.

I'd said I'd drive us to Manchester but I wasn't totally sure my old banger would make it. It's blue. That was the only reason I bought it. Kev backed me up at the time. I'd taken him along because he used to work on the production line at a Land Rover factory.

"You should get it," he'd said.

"Is it sound mechanically?" I'd asked him.

"Yeah, I reckon. And it's Shelby Town blue. That's the main thing. I've always wanted a blue car."

"Why don't *you* buy one, then?"

"Nah, no, no…" he'd said and that was the end of that.

So I bought the blue car and Kev was thrilled. He has a perfectly good Mondeo, but when it came to driving to away games, he always says he will and then somehow never does.

I'd arranged to meet Kev, Inchy and Tyson outside Carphone Warehouse on the High Street. Kev always wants to meet there as it's opposite the Town Hall. And that's where the Shelby players will go for a civic reception with the mayor when they win the FA Cup. That's Kev's fantasy, anyway, and he's almost become superstitious about making that our meeting point.

Inchy is huge and it's always a problem deciding where to put him in the car. If he sits in the back, then the other person is squashed. If he sits in the front next to me, then I can't see the wing mirror on his side. I ask him if anything is coming up on the inside, but he's so big he can't turn his neck enough to see.

Tyson has only started coming to Shelby games since they made it to the Premier League. Me and Kev always have a go at him about it. We ask him Shelby

Town trivia questions, which he could never hope to answer. And we still tease him about being a Leeds fan when we were at school. It's hard to believe but, back then, Leeds got as far as the Champions League semi-final and he never stopped going on about it, even though he'd never been to Elland Road. After Leeds nearly bankrupted themselves and passed Shelby going up as they went down, Tyson mysteriously changed allegiance. Of course that just meant he'd never been a proper Leeds fan in the first place.

I pulled up outside Carphone Warehouse and there was Kev, staring longingly at the mobiles in the window. He loves gadgets, especially phones. He reckons all Premier League footballers have two phones: one to ring their wives on, and one to ring their girlfriends. I said that was rubbish. What about Dave Morgan? He'd never be unfaithful to Mrs Morgan. Kev said that was a fair point but that he *needed* to have a second mobile, even if the club captain didn't. If you ask me, Kev is just addicted to gadgets.

I knew Kev would be early. He's always early. For home games, he'll turn up an hour or two before kick-off and then walk around saying hello to all the people selling flags and scarves, hot dogs and burgers, programmes and scratch cards. He reckons all those people work incredibly hard, because every time he approaches one of them they puff out their cheeks, blow quite hard and then looked really busy.

Then Tyson appeared, strolling along with a great big beige beanie over his dreadlocks and a set of speakers over the top, the size of teacups.

"I'm going to ask him one early. To wake him up." Kev grinned. "All right, T? When was the last time Shelby—"

"I can't hear ya, Kev," lied Tyson, indicating the headphones.

"What are you listening to?" I asked him.

"What?" said Tyson, peeling off his speakers and lifting one side of his beanie. "Tinchy Stryder, innit?"

"Tinchy's a silly name," said Kev.

"Speaking of which, have you seen Inchy?" I asked.

"What?" said Tyson again.

I thought of Dave's "herding cats" comparison as I directed T and Kev into the blue car.

"Inchy'll be at the café," I said, starting the engine.

Sure enough, there he was, sitting in the window of the café down the road, eating like his life depended on it. He likes to sit there because, although the seats are bolted down, like in the rest of the café, the table at the window has a bit more legroom.

He didn't notice us pull up, so Kev went up to the glass and stared right at him.

"Oi!" he shouted, "Tinchy Stryder!"

Inchy jumped, knocking a mushroom off his plate, which rolled across the table and onto the floor, despite his best efforts to stop it. He dragged himself out from behind the table and hurried out to the car.

"You missed a 'shroom there, mate," said Kev.

"Yeah, whose fault is that?" he grumbled.

"Come on, Inchy," I said. "I told you one o'clock outside Carphone Warehouse."

"Sorry, mate. Lunchtime. I had to start early this morning so my boss would let me have the afternoon off," he said, squeezing himself into the back seat next to Tyson.

"What are you listening to, T?"

"Tinchy Stryder."

"Silly name," said Inchy.

And we set off.

The Carling Cup gets a bad press and some
people say it's a Mickey Mouse competition,
but when Shelby Town reached the final in
their first season in the Premier League,
Kev and I agreed it was *The Greatest Day of Our Lives.*
Even if we were battered by Arsenal. At least we were
in the lead for a while. For Shelby Town, being in the
lead against Arsenal at Wembley was way beyond
fantasy. I'd looked at Kev at one point and he actually
had his eyes shut, his head tipped back.

"You all right, mate?"

"I'm just listening to it, mate. It's amazing."

I shut my eyes too, and it *was* truly amazing.
A cacophony of Shelby Town songs, rolling over one
another. Only the sound of Inchy choking on his hot
dog as Arsenal equalized woke us from our reverie.
Tyson, meanwhile, was leading the singing. He's
brilliant at making up Shelby chants, although they
don't always catch on.

"No one can handle these rhymes of my times, you
get me?" he'll shout.

Anyway, we were desperate to get to Wembley again this year, and the Carling Cup was our best hope. The trouble was it meant us driving hundreds of miles on a Wednesday afternoon, and Kev and Inchy having to get time off work. Tyson is at college so he was all right. I work at the library, running workshops for kids who have trouble reading. They're fun but really I want to be a writer. A football writer.

We stopped halfway to get petrol. Tyson had been asleep in the back with his headphones on, and we knew he'd moan.

"What did you stop here for?" he whined. "This one's rubbish."

"It's a petrol station, T. They all get their sandwiches from the same vast sandwich-making company in Wales."

"Do they?"

"No, I made it up," said Kev. "But I will get you the sandwich of your choice if you can tell me which Shelby Town players were ever-present in our run to the Carling Cup final."

"I'll get my own," muttered Tyson, slipping out of the car seat and across the forecourt like a cat.

Inchy was already at the counter. "Early start for me today," he was telling the woman serving. "I'm starving."

"What's the vegetarian special?" I asked, pointing at a sign saying "Vegetarian Special Available".

"Tuna melt," she said curtly.

"That's not vegetarian," I told her.

"I'll get my supervisor," she said and disappeared.

Inchy began to panic. "She won't serve us now!"

"What's he done this time?" said Kev, coming over. "You being a radical activist?"

"No," I said. "Just a vegetarian."

The supervisor appeared. "Vegetarians eat fish and white meat," he told us.

"'Course they do," laughed Kev. "'Cos those are the nicest vegetables."

After I'd paid for the petrol, me, Kev and Tyson went and sat in the car to wait for Inchy. When he finally appeared, we watched him set off across the forecourt in the wrong direction.

"Oi!" shouted Tyson.

"No, leave it, T. Let's see what he does," Kev said with a grin.

Inchy walked over to a blue saloon car on the opposite side of the petrol station, opened the door and worked his frame into the passenger's seat. No sooner had he shut the door than he immediately opened it again. We'd never seen him move so fast. He spun round looking for us as we fell about laughing.

"Come on, Inchy!" I shouted.

He rushed over and got in the car, panting and frowning.

"Why did you move the car?" he said crossly.

"We didn't!" we said together, then all four of us fell about laughing again.

"I got you a vegetable pasty," said Inchy finally, handing me a greasy bag.

"Thanks, mate," I said.

It was quite a drive from Shelby to Manchester, and it was dark by the time we got to the outskirts. As we drove through Salford, on the west of the city, we could make out the vast structure that was Old Trafford: Manchester United's home, with its floodlights blazing, ready for the night's game.

"Evil Empire, three o'clock!" declared Kev, and we all stared out at the forbidding monolith in the distance.

"Who they got tonight?" said Tyson.

"Newcastle."

"Is Dave going?" Kev asked me.

"I asked him and he just said, 'Do I look stupid?'" I replied.

"He'll be staying home with Josie then," said Tyson. "He's no fool. Why come an' watch his team get bashed up when he can slide on your couch with your fit sister?"

"Yes, thank you, T. Josie's got kick-boxing tonight, actually."

"How far is it to Bury from here then?" asked Inchy, changing the subject.

"Eleven point nine miles according to the sat nav," said Kev. "And that's five different satellites tracking you, Inchy. These things are amazing."

Bury's home ground is Gigg Lane and we'd arranged to meet some other Shelby fans in a nearby pub called The Pack Horse. It was an hour 'til kick-off and Kev fancied a bit of banter before the game. Tyson ordered a ginger ale, which he knew made him stand out from everyone else, just the way he liked it. Inchy asked around and found out there was a chippy round the corner, so he went off to "grab a snack".

It felt odd for Shelby fans to be back at Gigg Lane. Bury were in League Two and when we first got in the league, playing there was a step up. Now we were the "big club" and Bury fancied a giant-killing.

"Tyson!" said Kev suddenly.

"What?"

"How long have Bury been playing at Gigg Lane?" Tyson gave him a look.

"Since 1885. How long's that?" said Kev, undeterred.

"Ages."

"It's 2013 now, so that's 128 years, isn't it? What are they teaching you at that college? Here's another one. Who did Bury beat in the FA Cup final in 1903, when their 6–0 win was the highest ever recorded in a Cup Final?"

Tyson rolled his eyes and turned to talk to Amanda, the red-haired girl we see at every Shelby away game. She knows all the trivia but doesn't make a big thing of it. I could hear him mouthing "Tinchy Stryder" at her as she reached to try on his headphones.

"Tyson?" said Kev.

"Derby County," I told him. "Now shut up and let's go in."

Shelby were hopeless in the first half and Kev was furious.

"Looks like the foreign boys don't fancy it up here against a League Two side in the pouring rain," he muttered.

"It's not raining. And Jean-Pierre Vert's our best player," I added.

I hate it when he gets angry with the team.

"We can't handle Ben Futcher at corners," he said. "Hey, T? Who was Ben Futcher's dad?"

"Mr Futcher," said Tyson, which made Amanda laugh. She whispered something in his ear.

"Son of Paul. Nephew of Ron," continued Tyson, smiling at Kev.

"*That* is the girl of my dreams," Kev said to me, staring wistfully at Amanda just as a Bury corner swung over and Ben Futcher crashed a header into the roof of the Shelby net.

"Right, that's it," said Kev. "I can never look at Amanda during a game again."

"What happened?" asked Inchy, returning from the pie stand with three chicken baltis and a cheese and onion parcel for me.

"You didn't get Amanda nothing?" demanded Tyson.

"Do girls eat pies?" replied Inchy.

"It's fine," said Amanda.

"Will you lot concentrate on the game? Some of us want to go back to Wembley," growled Kev, trying not to look at Amanda. Which just made him look a bit mad.

The second half began with Town still one down. And now it *was* raining.

"Told you," said Kev.

The Bury fans started singing, "Premier League?

You're having a laugh!" and the Shelby fans were very quiet.

"SING UP!" yelled Tyson.

"Shall we sing a song for you?" jeered the Bury supporters, just as a Dave Morgan back pass got stuck in the mud. A pile of bodies – goalkeeper, defenders and Bury strikers – slid towards the ball and it popped up, bounced and spun freakishly into the goal. 2–0 to Bury.

"Go–o–o home! You might as well go home!" sang the whole of Gigg Lane.

Dave Morgan seemed to take the song personally and surged forwards, clipping the ball to Dotun Odegbame, who touched it back into the skipper's path. It was a perfect lay-off from the Nigerian and Dave instantly detonated a twenty-five-yarder past the Bury keeper. 2–1 now, but with only a minute to go. We could see Mick Diamond, Shelby's manager, frantically whistling at the Town subs, who were warming up.

"Get Dolan on!" shouted Kev.

Sure enough, Mick was pointing at Stuart Dolan, who couldn't have stripped off quicker if his tracksuit had been on fire, and on he came. He ran across the Bury backline as a long ball was hit deep into their half. Dotun challenged big Ben Futcher and the ball landed behind them. Dolan pounced, quick as a whippet. He looked at the keeper, stamped his right foot down as if to shoot and then lifted the ball into the net with his left. The keeper dived the wrong way. 2–2!

There was pandemonium in the away end. Inchy hugged me and Kev until we could hardly breathe. Tyson was on his knees praying. Amanda jumped and screamed. She had been at school with Stuart Dolan. The referee blew for full-time. A draw.

But this was the Carling Cup.

"Extra time," said Inchy. "Does anyone want some crisps?"

The extra half-hour was played out but with no more goals. The Bury players were struggling as the fitter Shelby lads began to control the game. Dotun hit the post, but we knew what was coming well before the end: penalties.

The shoot-out was at our end. Bury went first and their poor lad skied the first kick up into the night air.

"That's gone out of the ground!" shouted Kev.

Our boys were superb, every penalty bulging the net in front of us. The next two exhausted Bury lads had their kicks saved, which meant that if Dotun scored our third, we'd be 3–0 up with two to go. The Shelby centre forward stopped in his run-up, causing the keeper to go down on one knee, and then side-footed into the net before standing in front of us, rocking and swaying in a relaxed and beautiful Nigerian dance. Tyson laughed and copied him while Dotun disappeared under a pile of teammates.

"We're on our way, mate!" cried Kev, turning to me. "You and me at Wembley again. Only two rounds and a semi-final to go."

We tumbled out of Gigg Lane, dancing off into the night, as the Lancashire police herded us down the Manchester Road in the direction of the town centre. I'm still not really sure what happened next, but half an hour later, after much singing and jostling, we slumped exhausted around a table on the Shelby Town

Football Special. I was asleep within seconds as the motion of the train rocked me into darkness. It was only when I woke up, somewhere near Birmingham, that I remembered the car. We'd *driven* to Bury, hadn't we? And now we were on our way back to Shelby by train. Extra time and a penalty shootout. We'd all gone a bit mad after but you'd have thought *one* of us could have remembered.

The lights were still on at home as I came up the path. As I opened the door, Josie called out, "That was a late one!"

"We won on penalties," I called back.

Dave came in from the kitchen. "Newcastle won at Old Trafford. Beat their reserves 2–1. We didn't hear you come up the road, mate. You finally had the exhaust fixed on that old banger of yours?"

"Er … yeah," I said.

"Thought you'd maybe left the car in Bury and got a lift back with the Massive Russian," said Josie, coming into the room.

"Don't be daft," I retorted, crossing my fingers in my pocket. I just hoped there'd be another game in the Manchester area in Round Four so I'd be able to go and pick up my car. My Shelby Blue car…

Ways to Celebrate

(Danny Smith's poem)

He's a shirt removin' crowd salutin'

handstandin' happy landin'

rockin' rollin' divin' slidin'

posin' poutin' loud shoutin'

pistol packin' smoke blowin'

flag punchin' kiss throwin'

hip swingin' arm wavin'

robot dancin' cool ravin'

shoulder shruggin' team huggin'

badge pointin' double jointin'

someraultin' hoardin' vaultin'

last-minute goal grinnin'

shoe shinin' shin spinnin'

celebratin' match-winnin' *STRIKER!*

the Winner

Other books you might enjoy...

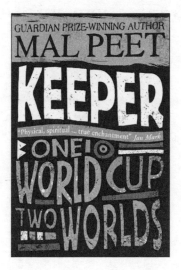

In a newspaper office, Paul Faustino, South
America's top sports journalist, sits opposite the
man they call El Gato – the Cat – the world's
greatest goalkeeper. On the table between them
is the World Cup…

El Gato tells his incredible story – how he,
a poor logger's son, became a World Cup-winning
goalkeeper. And, finally, Faustino learns of the
mysterious Keeper, who haunted a football pitch
at the heart of the claustrophobic forest, the man
who taught El Gato his amazing skills.

ISBN 978-1-4063-3829-4

Megan Fawcett turns up every week to
football practice, but does Mr Glasshouse
ever pick her for the team?
Nope.

The only way Megan can play is
to form her own team – a girls-only team.

Luckily a chance meeting with the captain
of the Parrs, a local women's football squad,
means they have someone to coach them.

And so the Parrs U11s are born...

ISBN 978-1-4063-1730-5

ALEX RIDER MISSION 1 : STORMBREAKER
ANTHONY HOROWITZ

NUMBER ONE BESTSELLING SERIES

When MI6 recognizes his potential,
Alex Rider is armed with secret gadgets
and sent on his first mission. But the teenage
spy soon finds himself in mortal danger.

His first assignment may well be his last…

"Cracking with suspense and daring." Guardian

ISBN 978-1-84428-092-6

A DOZEN DEVILISH TALES

Man-eating massage chairs; terrifying train rides with
the living dead; sinister sat navs that direct you to
your doom – how many grisly ways are there to die?

This collection displays the dazzling wit
and wicked humour of the master storyteller
Anthony Horowitz. It is guaranteed to make
your blood curdle and your spine tingle.

SOMETIMES YOUR NIGHTMARES BECOME REAL...

ISBN 978-1-4063-2561-4